CHRISTMAS AT COZY HOLLY INN

PINECONE FALLS BOOK 1

MEREDITH SUMMERS

CHAPTER 1

"*V*ermont can't be that bad. I bet it's pretty with all the snow."

Julie Green frowned at the static coming from the Bluetooth speakers. Her friend Cheryl was trying to be supportive, but she sensed doubt in her voice. She couldn't blame her—snow was pretty in pictures and Christmas movies, but not so much when you had to drive in it.

"That's because you're not trying to navigate in all this whiteness. I can't even see where the roads are." Julie's knuckles were white on the steering wheel. She hunched close to the windshield, a posture that was driving nails into her shoulders, in the hopes of finding the edges of the turnoff she was looking for. "I'm just glad I rented something with four-wheel drive."

The Bluetooth speakers crackled. Cheryl's voice cut in and out, leaving only snatches of the conversation. "What... can't hear..."

Darn it! She'd overshot the turn. Understandable since the roads were hardly plowed and the access road to the inn was narrow. This was what she got for agreeing to return to the middle of nowhere—also known as Pinecone Falls—to help her grandmother host one last Christmas Eve party. Gram had been famous for them before she'd shut down the family inn and moved to a retirement community.

"What?" Cheryl said again, unhelpfully.

"Nothing," Julie shouted. Not that shouting would help cover the distance from Pinecone Falls, Vermont, to her home in Boston. "I'm in the middle of nowhere. The signal must be cutting out."

Snatches of static colored Cheryl's next words, but as Julie eased the truck into reverse and then turned into the unplowed drive of the family inn, at least she managed to catch a full sentence this time.

"Maybe you should have stayed in Boston."

"Right, because the one thing that would make this year better after losing my job would be to spend Christmas alone."

She held her breath and squinted through the windshield. Somewhere short of state lines, the wipers had left a smear across the glass, and she'd run out of windshield wiper fluid. She would grab more in Pinecone Falls when she went for a grocery run, but in the meantime, it left her squinting like a little old lady instead of the confident, thirty-two-year-old woman she was. If she could navigate Boston in rush hour, these back roads should be a piece of cake.

Should be. Her front passenger-side tire slipped off the winding drive and into the ditch. Fortunately, she was going at a crawl, and the four-wheel drive had no trouble compensating when she corrected back onto the unseen path. The mounds of fresh, white snow looked fluffy and inviting—until she had to drive through them. She'd give anything for Boston streets right now. Not that it didn't snow down there, but at least they plowed. The city streets never seemed to accumulate that much of it unless there was a huge storm, and then she'd simply take the bus to work.

"Don't you worry about your job," Cheryl said.

"It's been four months since *Boston Best* downsized and kicked me to the curb. I think I have the right to worry a little."

A burst of static drowned out the beginning of Cheryl's next sentence, but she ended with, "...put in a good word for you. I'm sure you're going to get a call from HR any day now."

Cheryl had jumped ship with *Boston Best* magazine long before Julie had noticed the signs that the magazine was on its way out. The fashion magazine Cheryl worked at now had an opening, and it was Julie's best hope at stable employment in the near future. If only Christmas wasn't less than two weeks away, with most management off work for the holidays.

"It's too close to Christmas. Maybe I'll get a call in January."

"Trust me, you'll get a call," Cheryl said, her emphatic tone heard even above the spotty cell phone service. "As long as you have the signal in Podunk, Vermont, to answer it!"

Julie smiled weakly and corrected around another bend in the road. Had the driveway been this long the last time she was here?

"If not, there's always email."

"Or you could come home, like a sane person."

That, Julie couldn't do. Gram had turned eighty years old this year. Although she had run the family bed-and-breakfast, the Cozy Holly Inn, into her seventies, about ten years ago, she'd made the difficult decision to shut down the business. Julie knew it had broken her heart. In a way, it had broken Julie's too. Even though she hadn't visited Pinecone Falls in years, she had fond memories of staying with her Gram and Gramps, when he was alive. She missed the simplicity of those years.

"I can't. I'm almost there."

The party wasn't even the real reason she couldn't go back to Boston with her tail between her legs, but she was afraid Cheryl would laugh if she knew the truth. When Gram had called and asked Julie to undertake this one last Christmas Eve party, she had sounded… fragile. The older Julie grew, the less time she seemed to have for visits with family. She didn't want to think about how much time she had left with Gram, especially now that she wasn't as active as she'd been while running the family inn.

"Okay, okay. I'll text you from civilization. Try to have a good time."

"Bye." Julie thumbed the button on the steering wheel to end the call. The beep echoed in the silent truck cab. The tension in her shoulders had mounted into screaming pain. With one hand on the steering wheel, she adjusted her position to stretch her back.

One last turn, and the inn came into view. Blankets of white bracketed the idyllic view. More snow dusted the steeply sloping roof. Painted a warm blue, the large, three-story house seemed almost asleep, nestled between snow-topped conifers. Icicles dripping from the roof caught the light, reminding Julie of how the inn would look once she strung Christmas lights outside. It was peaceful. Gorgeous.

But as she drew the truck to a stop in front of the

steps, the reality became apparent. Paint had chipped off the covered porch stairs and some of the siding. A shutter on one of the lower windows hung crooked. The banister looked askew. And that was just what she saw at first glance. Julie sighed and leaned her forehead against the steering wheel. The vibrations of the engine started to give her a headache. She shut off the truck.

"Maybe not so magical, then."

But she could work with it. Gram had given her the phone number of a carpenter in Pinecone Falls who was an old friend and ready to come out to the inn as soon as she called. She would load the porch with Christmas lights. The party was at night and in the dark, so no one would notice the need for a fresh coat of paint. All she had to do was decorate the house and confirm the catering that Gram had already set up. No problem.

Weary from the drive, Julie opened the door and jumped down into snow that came up to her knees. She yelped as the cold seeped around, into, and through her expensive suede boots. What had been adequate footwear for the shoveled sidewalks of Boston wouldn't last her thirty minutes in Pinecone Falls. Shivering, she rounded the truck to get her suitcase.

As she ducked under the low-hanging branch of a

pine tree to get there, a heap of snow plopped off the branch, hit her neck, and then slid down the back of her jacket.

"Great. Just great." Julie fervently hoped that this wouldn't be an omen of her trip. One way or another, she was stuck here in the middle of nowhere, with questionable cell phone service, for the next ten days.

Her trip was not off to the best start.

CHAPTER 2

The well-packed snow of the drive crunched beneath the wheels of Nolan Miller's truck as he pulled into his customary parking spot in front of Barrington Lodge. The rustic bed-and-breakfast, run by his family, could have been an old-world hunting lodge for an American tycoon. In fact, it might well have started out that way. The mansion, built in the 1850s by a railroad tycoon by the name of Homer Barrington, was built of hand-hewn cedar logs and river stone, with sprawling stables nestled behind it. Nolan had grown up here over summers spent with his grandfather, who had inherited the property from his grandfather. Someday, Nolan would carry on that family legacy.

For now, he hopped out of the truck and grabbed the sack of dog food he'd gone into town to pick up.

Despite its bulk, he hefted it easily onto his shoulder and walked along the shoveled stone path to the side entrance of the house. This was the entrance the family used, far removed from the more impressive lobby with its decorations of antlers, taxidermy trout, landscape oil paintings of old Vermont, and the dark-wood desk for greeting guests.

The side entrance was narrower, barely wide enough to accommodate Nolan's shoulders with the bag of dog food. By the time he shut the door behind him and kicked off his snow-crusted boots, the hall was made even narrower by the enormous dog running to greet him. The husky was almost entirely white, had more fur than muscle or fat, and thumped the ground with her tail as she sat politely to wait for Nolan's attention.

"Hi, Snowball." Nolan greeted his dog with a scratch around the ears. "Come on, now. I need to get to the kitchen."

Kitchen just so happened to be one of the words that made the husky's triangular ears perk up in delight. The dog turned on her heel and bounded down the hall. Nolan stopped by the storage room just off the kitchen to deposit the dog food. When he straightened, Snowball was standing in the doorway, giving him a disapproving look.

He laughed. "Come here, girl."

Wagging her tail, she trotted over to him so he could give her a proper scratch. She wiggled as he did. Despite the fact that it was winter, he still somehow ended up with a handful of dog fur. He stuffed it in the grapevine nesting ball that he would put out in spring. It was filled with hair and lint for the birds to use for nesting material. Nolan was always careful to only use natural shampoos on Snowball's fur so it wouldn't be toxic to the birds.

"Don't worry. You know I brought you a treat."

The husky nearly managed to trip him as he backtracked to the door to remove his outerwear and the package he'd put into his pocket. She danced in front of him the entire way to the kitchen, making the trip double the length it should have taken, but he didn't mind. Her excitement made him glad for his forethought.

In the kitchen, he found Gramps sitting at the table with a newspaper open in front of him and his reading glasses perched on his nose. Klaus Miller was less of an imposing man than he had been twenty years ago, with his receding hairline and his shoulders bowed from age. He would be eighty next year, and although he still commanded just as much of Nolan's and his father's obedience in running Barrington Lodge, Nolan had started to notice the way Gramps's clothes were fitting looser over his once-prominent belly.

Nolan paused. The tightening of his fingers around the brown paper wrapping made it crinkle. Nowhere in this house were any signs of the impending Christmas season, aside from the snow. The décor was the same as the rest of the year—no evergreen boughs or decorations hanging from the ceiling, and definitely no Christmas tree. After the passing of Nolan's mother, Mary, on Christmas Day three years past, Gramps pretended that the Christmas season didn't exist. So did Nolan's father, Stan. He'd destroyed years of family Christmas photos in his grief, photos that Nolan still mourned. He'd loved his mom as much as the two older men, but unlike them, he blamed cancer, not the Christmas season, for taking her from them.

A whine from near his knee reminded him of Snowball's patience. Feeling awkward, he hastily unwrapped the treat, a dog cookie decorated like a Christmas wreath, and offered it to her. She gobbled it down, but not before Gramps caught sight of the contraband holiday treat and gave a disapproving grunt.

Nolan rolled his neck to free himself of the tension climbing into his shoulders. "I saw a truck turn into the drive of the Cozy Holly Inn. Are you expecting an inspector today?"

With their longtime business rival having closed the business, Gramps had decided to purchase the property to expand Barrington Lodge. The two properties neighbored one another, albeit with a forest of evergreens in between and only a forest path joining the two, but they could widen that for vehicle use.

Gramps folded the newspaper and set it down next to a cup of coffee he'd probably reheated a half-dozen times already today. "No. We're finished with inspections on the property. Must be a tourist. Maybe they got lost looking for our place."

Snowball finished the last crunch of her cookie and hunted on the floor for crumbs she'd missed.

"The driveway's snowed over. Even GPS won't accidentally turn one of our customers down that way."

Gramps shook out the newspaper, a clear indication that the conversation was at an end. He'd been like this ever since his daughter—Nolan's mom—had passed, not talking much except when he had something he wanted to prove. In some ways, Nolan suspected he made things worse—he had his mom's eyes and her black hair. She had been the glue holding their family together, and all his attempts to fill the hole she'd left only worked halfway.

Dismissively, Gramps said, "Don't worry about it. Whoever's at the inn will find their way here before long. They're closed. Even if they make it through the door, the place is falling off its hinges."

Nolan sighed. "I guess I'll go check that we have a room, then."

Gramps didn't answer, but Snowball trotted after him as he left the kitchen.

CHAPTER 3

The interior of the inn was dark, cold, and dusty. Julie decided not to remove her boots. Her feet were like ice, but she suspected that the floorboards wouldn't be much better. She left her suitcase by the door and fumbled for the light switch, thankful that her grandmother had made sure the water, electricity, and heat were turned on before her arrival.

The first switch her hand found didn't work. She flicked it on, then off, then on again before cursing under her breath. A grope farther along the wall found a second switch near the first. This one brought light crackling to the small light fixture over her head. Thank goodness! If the inn hadn't had electricity, Julie really would have run back to Boston.

The floorboards creaked under her steps as she

continued past the coat hooks and dusty mirror—
which threw back the distorted reflection of a woman
with short, dirty-blond hair and an oval face—and
through the short corridor into the house proper.
She'd always been comfortable at the Cozy Holly Inn
in part because it hadn't felt like most B&Bs she'd
stayed at over the years. It felt more like a home than
an establishment, and that was reflected in the layout
of the house. Most of the downstairs consisted of an
enormous dining room to feed the guests staying in
one of the inn's eight rooms, but near the front door
was the cozy little nook the family had used as a living
room.

She found the light switch to this room quicker. It
illuminated haunted, sheet-covered shapes of furniture. The back of her neck prickled, and her breath
fogged up in front of her face. She needed to find the
thermostat and crank on the heat.

There was one in the living room, but she nearly
tripped over something sticking out from under one
of the sheets. Muttering under her breath, she fiddled
with the knob until she heard the rattle of the furnace
kicking in. Then she tackled the offending item under
the sheet.

Her grandfather's rocker. All Julie's rancor melted
away as she saw the sturdy, if scratched, chair. Each
of those scratches told a story, and she couldn't help

but run her finger along one of the deepest grooves. That one the chair had acquired from Julie when she'd been young and running through the house. Gram and Gramps hadn't been angry at her for knocking it over and adding to the map of small scars the chair held. Instead, they'd been more concerned that Julie had hurt herself, though she'd been afraid of their reproach, crying at the time. More memories trickled back to her as she moved on to the other, less noticeable scratches in the wood. Gramps reading to her as she sat on his lap or the floor. Gram sitting in her chair and knitting or working on a quilt.

Julie turned, and the next sheet-covered lump she revealed turned out to be Gram's chair. The upholstery was faded, the flowers in the once-white chair now faded into beige along with the rest of it. The other couch was newer and didn't hold the same memories, but Julie's throat still felt tight as she piled all the sheets in the room into a bundle for the laundry.

She shut her eyes and breathed deeply. Instead of the warm memory of the way the inn had smelled, she got a lungful of dust. As she doubled over, coughing, she couldn't help but think wryly, *There goes that happy nostalgic feeling.*

Gramps wasn't around anymore. Gram had

moved on to a retirement home. There was nothing in this big, drafty house but ghosts.

When she could breathe again, Julie straightened and continued with the pile of sheets through the house in search of others to add to it.

The back parlor still had the comfy furniture and fireplace that guests loved. The dining room still had the giant server, chain cabinet, and mahogany table long enough for sixteen guests. All the chairs were now upside down on the top of the table. She left the chairs up. Cleaning the floors would have to be one of the first things on her to-do list.

As she turned away from the dining room, she paused. Was that a noise?

"It's just a creaky old house, Julie. There aren't actually any ghosts here."

But there it came again, a vigorous scratching she might have attributed to the wind or branches hitting the windowpanes, except it seemed to be coming from *inside* the house.

She dropped her sheet bundle and armed herself with the contents of her pockets, which turned out to be a wad of unused tissues and a tube of lip gloss. In other words, useless. The sound came again. Julie held her breath as she tiptoed forward. Her wet boots found a creaky spot on the floor, and she froze, listening.

Was someone else in the house with her?

A loud ringing trumpeted through the air, and Julie yelped. It took a full thirty seconds for her to recognize the sound as her cell phone. She shoved her hands into her coat pockets again, only to come up empty. It must have fallen out.

Maybe that was what had been scratching—or rather, vibrating against the floor with incoming text messages. She did *not* have the patience to talk to Cheryl again right now. If her friend told her to pack up and drive back to Boston, Julie might just do it.

She found her phone next to Gram's chair and wiped the dusty screen on her pants before she answered it.

"Mom?" Her voice held more relief than she'd wanted to let leak through.

"Julie? Can you hear me?"

The line held more than a little static, but it was better than when she had been speaking with Cheryl earlier. Julie raised her voice. "Yes, Mom. Can you hear me?"

"Yes. Oh, we really need to hook up the landline in that house. The cell signal is terrible."

"You can say that again," Julie quipped. She was glad to hear from her mom, Margaret. She didn't get to see her parents often because they spent their time jetting around the world so her mother could attend art galleries, teach classes, and create more of the art that her fans called masterpieces. Even though her parents weren't around, they kept in touch with frequent phone and FaceTime calls.

"Did you make it to the inn okay?"

"Yes. Just pulled in a couple minutes ago."

"How was the drive?" another voice shouted. Her dad, Gregory. Her parents must have her on speakerphone.

Great, until I left civilization and recently plowed roads. Julie bit back her sarcasm and answered, "Fine. It's just starting to snow here."

"Oh, the inn is so beautiful in the winter."

Her mom sounded wistful.

The scratching sound came again, almost as if it was wistful too.

"On the outside, sure," Julie grumbled. "Inside, it's like a bad scary movie."

"What was that?"

She sighed. "Nothing. The house is just making some weird creaking sounds. I'm going to check it out."

"Don't go in the basement," her dad joked.

"Ha ha." He wasn't helping her mood.

Bracing herself, Julie followed the sound into the

kitchen. The static on the line cleared—apparently, the signal was better in here. The sound came again. Not a scratching, exactly. A rattling.

"Is something in the basement?"

"Probably a serial killer," Dad joked. "Take a baseball bat."

"Oh, Greg, that isn't funny. Stop that! I'm sure it's nothing."

Julie hoped her mom was right. "You're right. It's probably just a draft. Do you want me to call you back?"

"No, no. Stay on the line. Did you get the list of things you need to do for the party?"

Julie crept closer to the closed basement door, her heart pounding. She barely heard herself as she answered, "Yep. Cleaning out the house should have been on the top of the list."

A sigh. "Well, it has been a couple years since Gram closed it up. I guess that's to be expected. There might be a maid service in town…"

In Pinecone Falls? Doubtful.

"It's fine. It'll give me something to do. I have ten days until the party, and it's not going to take that long to straighten out the catering and decorate."

"If you're sure…"

When she was inches from the door, it gave another rattle.

"What was that?"

Apparently, the noise could be heard even over the phone.

"The basement door."

Her dad joked, "Just like in all the scary movies."

"Oh, Greg, you are not helping."

Julie took a deep breath. This was Pinecone Falls; nothing ever happened here. It was probably just a mouse. And if that were the case, she should check it out. It wouldn't do to have mice running around at the party.

She reached for the basement door and yanked it open.

Meooururuw!

A ball of fur exploded from the basement and past her, out of the kitchen. Julie's yelp was strangled in her throat.

"Julie? Jules, are you there?" Her dad's voice sounded worried. For all his teasing about what was in the basement, he really was concerned for her.

She cleared her throat and said, "Yep. Some kind of wild animal, I think."

"So not a serial killer."

"Try not to sound disappointed, Dad."

Mom interjected, "You should call animal control. Don't confront it. It could be dangerous."

"Good idea." Julie doubted that animal control

came out right away here in the middle of nowhere, and she wouldn't be able to sleep with a wild animal running around the house. Hopefully, she could shoo it outside. She grabbed the first thing she found under the sink, which happened to be a plunger.

What kind of animal had it been? It had run past too fast for her to tell.

Slowly, on her tiptoes, she crept along after it. Her parents were nattering on in her ear, but she barely heard them between the renewed static and her thumping heart. When she reached the living room, she caught sight of a lump of fur in the shadow of Gram's chair, licking its white fur clean of dust.

She lowered the plunger and set it against the wall. "Oh, it's a cat."

"A cat?" Clearly, she'd interrupted her mom in the middle of saying something, but she hadn't been paying enough attention to know what.

"The wild animal. It must be a stray." And that explained the noise. Julie relaxed, even though this only added to her problems. She couldn't throw a cat out into the cold snow to fend for itself. It would be wrong.

As if knowing the bend of her thoughts, the cat glared at her with brilliant-blue eyes. She crouched, holding out her fingers for the cat to sniff. "Here, kitty, kitty." She clucked under her tongue.

The cat looked her over as if she was a lesser being.

In her ear, her mother laughed, the sound half-covered with static. "You always did love cats. Remember Whiskers? You used to take that cat with you everywhere, even up to the inn in the summers!"

Whiskers hadn't looked that different from this cat. Well, she might have, once this cat was properly cleaned. Whiskers had been a gray cat with white markings without being covered in years' worth of basement dust. This one could be any color underneath all that dirt, though Julie suspected it was mostly white.

A pang of longing shot through her. She'd loved that cat and still missed her to this day. But after Whiskers had died, she'd gotten busy with college and then making her way in the world with her first jobs. Her apartment in Boston didn't allow for pets, and even filling it with plants on every spare surface hadn't quite filled that hole. But there was no sense in getting attached to this cat. She'd be going back home and wouldn't be able to keep it. She straightened and returned to the kitchen to lean against the counter, where the cell signal was better.

"What am I going to do with it?"

She realized that she'd interrupted her parents'

reminiscences of their old cat only at the awkward silence. She cleared her throat.

"Sorry, my mind's miles away. I moved back to the kitchen where I have better cell signal. What were you saying?"

While she waited for her parents to answer, she chewed on a thumbnail.

"I don't see why this is a problem," her dad said. "You love cats. Probably the only grandchildren I'm likely to get."

Julie sighed. Her parents had recently started mentioning grandchildren, but Julie was in no hurry. She was only thirty-two, and there was plenty of time, wasn't there? "Just because I'm not dating anyone right now doesn't mean I never will, Dad."

Her mom said, "Stop teasing, Greg. She's clearly had a long day." Julie opened her mouth to thank her mom for the intervention, only to have her mom add, "But I do agree with him, Jules. You love cats."

"I don't live here. I can't keep it."

The cat, in that uncanny way felines had of knowing when they were unwanted, slinked into the doorway. It had managed to clean itself until it was mostly white again, with only a bit of dusky gray on the muzzle. It glared at her and swished its tail.

"Well, there's an animal shelter in town. Your gram's friend, Myrtle, runs it, if I remember right."

Julie pulled the phone away from her ear to check the time. After five o'clock. "I don't suppose it's open late."

"Probably not, no…"

"And how am I supposed to get the cat there? I can't take it in the truck. It's a rental. What if the cat scratches up the seats?"

She was starting to get a headache. As if she didn't have enough problems already, now she was going to have to go into town and hope there was a pet store to buy a cat carrier.

Thankfully, her mother came to the rescue. "Oh, you know Gram. She never throws anything out. I bet one of Whiskers's old cat carriers is in the attic."

"Perfect. I'll look now. The signal here isn't great, so I'm going to let you go."

"Let us know how it goes tomorrow," Mom said.

"And give a kiss to my furry grandchild for me," Dad joked.

"Very funny, Dad. Love you both."

"You, too, dear!" her parents chorused.

Julie hung up the phone and stared at the cat.

If this was how her stay was starting, it was going to be a very long ten days.

CHAPTER 4

A set of narrow, steep stairs led to the attic. Dust covered every step. As a child, the big attic had been a place to explore. It was the whole top floor of the house, with dormer windows and filled with cast-off furniture and boxes loaded with all kinds of old treasures. And spiders.

As she hesitated at the bottom of the rickety staircase, she caught a flash of white fur from the corner of her eye. The cat had followed her. Crouching down on her heels, Julie reached out a hand, hoping to coax it forward. The creature shied away instead. She sighed. She hadn't been able to get it to warm to her when she'd unpacked her suitcase and found sheets—thankfully sealed in storage containers and free of dust—for the bed.

You don't want it to warm to you. You aren't going to keep it.

All true, but it would be nice to stop thinking of the cat as an "it" in her head.

Turning away, she muttered under her breath, "You probably know I'm trying to get rid of you." Cats were uncanny that way.

It followed her up to the attic. There were lots of cobwebs, but she didn't see any spiders. Maybe because it was frigid up here. Although the heat had been circulating for an hour by now, it apparently hadn't made its way into the attic.

As she stood looking at the mismatched chairs and old bureaus, she felt like she was a kid again. The attic still looked the same, still had that smell of dry wood. She peeked inside a cardboard box, using the flashlight of her phone for light.

The light of her flashlight reflected back at her against glittering strands. A gold garland for the Christmas tree. She couldn't help but smile as she opened the box fully and tallied the contents. More garlands, holly, mistletoe, and a hideously snarled string of lights. The next box held more of the same, and the third held ornaments carefully wrapped in newspaper.

"At least I won't have to buy anything for the

party." It looked as though Gram had everything she would need right here.

But where was that cat carrier?

She made her way past old frames, kitchen chairs, cardboard boxes, and plastic bins until finally, wedged into the corner, she found the cat carrier. She pulled it out in triumph.

"Look. Your new home!"

The cat, of course, was nowhere to be seen. Well, Julie wasn't heartless enough to leave the poor thing in the carrier overnight. She would have to catch it in the morning.

She made her way to the stairs with the cat carrier, glancing at the boxes of decorations on the way past. She'd have to come back for those. Three boxes of decorations, an entire house to clean and decorate, plus the catering and repairs to organize. It would be a lot of work, but Julie had insisted on setting things up ahead of Gram's arrival. She didn't want her grandmother to overwork herself.

"This isn't going to be as easy as I thought it would be, is it?"

From her vantage point, she could just see the top of the cat's ears poking up from the staircase. The ears twitched.

"Don't worry. I'm not going to ask you to help, even if you would make a good duster."

Her only answer was the swish of a fluffy tail as the cat turned around and quickly stalked off.

As she headed down the stairs, her phone rang. This time, it was Gram. Julie smiled as she answered it.

"Hi, Gram."

"Julie, honey. Did you get to the inn safely?"

"Yes. No trouble. You sound better."

"D-do I?" Gram devolved into a coughing fit.

Julie's chest constricted. Maybe she'd spoken too soon. The coughing went on much longer than she'd hoped. So long, in fact, that it almost seemed a bit forced. But that was silly. Gram wouldn't fake being sick—why would she? Except wasn't that the reason that Julie had finally agreed to host one last party? Gram had asked her a few times over the years, and she'd always said no. But this time with Gram being sick, she couldn't refuse.

When Gram stopped long enough to catch her breath, Julie said, "Are you sure you're going to be okay to make the trip here for the party with Mom and Dad?"

"What? Yes, of course. It's just a little tickle in my throat. Don't you dare tell them otherwise."

Julie could picture Gram's steady glare, but it didn't make her feel any better.

"Maybe you should go to the hospital and get that

cough checked out. You might have a chest infection."

"It's nothing, I promise. And I don't want you to tell your parents otherwise. You know they'll cut short Margaret's big trip, and she'll miss her gallery opening. That's more important."

Gram was still as stubborn as always.

"How's the house?" Gram asked, changing the subject. "I hope you're able to find everything you need."

"I just found the Christmas decorations, so everything is going great." Julie decided not to mention how dusty and run-down the place was. The run-down part she might not be able to do anything about, but she would be cleaning it until she could see her reflection in the hardwood floors so it would be perfect for Gram. "Oh, and you'll never believe what happened!"

"Oh? What happened?"

"I found a cat in the basement."

"A cat? You don't say. I wonder how it got in."

She didn't sound particularly surprised. Julie tried not to take that as an omen. If a cat could find its way in through the basement, what else could crawl in there?

Resigned, she said, "I'll check the basement for

broken windows or holes. Maybe it came in through the old bulkhead or something."

"Don't you worry about it. I'm sure Bob can handle it. Have you called him yet?"

"Not yet. I'm waiting until morning. But I will, don't worry."

"Good."

"And I'm bringing the cat to the shelter in the morning too. Mom said your friend Myrtle runs it?"

"Myrtle!" Gram exclaimed then started coughing again.

Julie pulled the phone away from her ear, holding her breath until Gram stopped. This time, the coughing fit didn't last long.

Gram continued the conversation as if it had never happened. "Oh, I miss Myrtle. Are you sure you want to bring the cat to her, though? It will be good for you to have something to keep you company out there."

Was that a joke? Julie was used to being alone. She lived alone in Boston, after all. What were a few days in a spooky house that seemed like it belonged in a scary movie?

But she actually didn't believe that. This was the family inn. As run-down as it had become, as eerie as it was to see it empty with sheets over the furniture and dust on the floor, it was still a place of fond memories for her. And for the rest of her family too. When she was little, they'd always spent Christmas here at the inn. It was family tradition.

Besides, Gram seemed to be trying to distract from that latest coughing fit. "I'm sure I'll be fine on my own," Julie said. Then, trying not to sound too patronizing, she added, "Maybe you should go to bed early tonight, Gram. Rest. And promise me if that coughing gets worse, you'll go to the hospital."

"I'm fine, honey. Absolutely fine. But I'll let you get back to your evening. Call if you need anything."

"I will," Julie promised. As she ended the call, an unsettling thought crept in. What if this was Gram's last Christmas?

If so, Julie had better put on a party worth remembering. Feeling sick with worry, she put the cat carrier on the second-floor landing and headed back up to the attic for the decorations. She had a lot of work to do.

CHAPTER 5

*J*ulie woke to silence. It was strange, not hearing the rumble of cars passing on the street, the angry calls from irritable people who hadn't had their coffee yet, the barks of dogs. Boston was a city in motion, and that motion started very early in the morning. Julie had learned to fall asleep to that white noise.

Pinecone Falls was different. When she'd crawled into bed, she'd found the silence so unusual, that she'd found an app on her phone of white noise to fall asleep to. Not that it had helped much. Her internet connection, connected to her phone signal, had cut in and out, stopping the sound at intervals for the silence to creep back in. Finally, she'd fallen asleep.

Maybe it wasn't entirely silent. If she strained her

ears, she heard steady, soft breathing. She stirred, and the breathing came closer, followed by a warm weight on her head. A cat's white, poufy tail batted at her face. Julie smiled. Maybe the cat was warming to her after all.

Sleepily, she stretched out an arm to pet the fluffy animal currently trying its best to suffocate her. The cat reared back, hind claws digging into Julie's cheek. She yelped. The cat bolted, its paws making a soft thud as it landed on the floor.

With that brilliant start to the day, she soon realized that the bathroom didn't have a first aid kit—she added it to her shopping list. The scratch wasn't deep and hadn't bled much, but she used toilet paper and water to clean it anyway. All this before coffee.

The house creaked as she dragged herself down the stairs to the kitchen. On her way, she'd stopped at a convenience store to get the essentials: instant coffee, creamer, and a box of white powdered donuts. She stuffed one into her mouth and chewed as she heated the coffee in the inn's ancient microwave.

Mew.

The small, desolate sound reminded her that she wasn't alone in the inn. She turned, eyeing the cat who now crouched in the doorway. It looked repentant, its big, luminous eyes reflecting the sunlight coming in through the kitchen window.

Mew.

It must be hungry. Cat food had not been on her shopping list, and it still wasn't, but she couldn't just leave him with nothing. She rinsed out the inner plastic container that had housed the donuts—the remnants now toppled onto the outer cardboard shell —and filled it with water. She hadn't considered the cat might need water and food... or other necessities.

She didn't even have a litter box in the house, which probably meant that she would be in for a fun surprise somewhere in the inn while she did the cleaning. One more reason why she needed to get rid of this cat.

When she lowered the container to the floor, the cat gingerly advanced on it. It lapped at the water, its hungry blue eyes never leaving her. Julie crumbled under the weight of those eyes. Did cats eat donuts? Hopefully, they weren't too unhealthy for them, but if this one had been living in the basement fending for itself, it had probably eaten less healthy things.

"You're going to get diabetes," she muttered as she broke pieces off the donut. She left them on the floor next to the container.

The cat gave her an imperious look as if to say, *What is this?* It nibbled at part of the donut anyway.

Funny thing, the cat did look pretty well-fed for a stray. And clean too. Hopefully, if someone owned it, they would check in with the animal shelter, where the cat would be after Julie dropped it off this morning.

The microwave beeped, and she retrieved her steaming mug of coffee. She cradled the white stoneware mug she'd taken from the cabinet between her palms and inhaled. It didn't feel like home, but it definitely made her morning better.

At least until she returned upstairs to find that her suede boots were utterly ruined. Grimacing, she snapped a picture of them and sent it to Cheryl. The picture message took forever to go through, but at least it did at last.

The reply arrived a minute later when she was fully dressed in yesterday's dusty jeans and a fresh sweater. She wished she'd thought to bring some older clothes for cleaning. Maybe she could pick up some cheap T-shirts in town. She checked her phone.

Cheryl: Reason #425 why Boston is better than Podunk, Vermont. Cleared sidewalks. No snow!!

With her boots mangled, Julie couldn't argue. Except the snow in Boston was closer to slush. It never really crystalized but lingered in the shadow of the sidewalks to splash onto your boots whenever a car passed.

One glance out the window showed a very different scene. Fields of white snow reflected the pink morning light like it was crusted with tiny diamonds. The trees near the house were capped with more snow. A red cardinal sat on the nearest branch, its chest puffed out. For a minute, Julie watched, captivated. When she tried to snap a picture, the cardinal flew away.

Oh, well. The window was probably too dirty to get a good picture, anyway.

Julie: The snow isn't *that* bad.

Cheryl: Don't get used to it.

Julie glanced again at her ruined boots. She shook her head.

Julie: No chance of that.

Cheryl: Good. Because I talked to HR, and I'm sure they're going to call you for an interview any time now.

Goodness, Julie hoped so. After an idyllic sort-of vacation in Vermont, the icing to cap off her trip would be to return home with a job lined up and her life back on track.

For now, she pulled on her boots and went to find the cat carrier. It was time to get rid of her unwanted guest.

❄

No amount of plaintive *mews* could convince Julie to keep this cat. She had a fresh set of scratches on her hands from coercing the little demon into the cat carrier. She was starving, having shared her stale breakfast, her feet were freezing despite having turned the heater on full blast, and her boots were ruined.

But as she reached the town proper, her sour mood started to fade. Frosted evergreen trees gave way to neat one- and two-story houses with painted shutters and Christmas decorations on the lawn. Julie slowed as she passed one house in particular that looked like a life-sized version of a gingerbread house. You didn't see things like that in Boston. At least, not on her apartment block.

The houses, in turn, gave way to shops interspersed by old-fashioned streetlamps decorated with swags of evergreens and wreaths with red bows. Each shop had added to the decorations in an eclectic but charming mishmash of candy canes, gingerbread men, Santas, and reindeer. The door to the pet store had cat toys hanging from the wreath, to match the plush cat with a Santa hat in the window display. Grinning, Julie checked her GPS as she continued past it. The animal shelter was on the other side of town, but considering how small Pinecone Falls was, and how prettily it was dressed up for Christmas, Julie didn't mind. The cat was silent in the carrier on the passenger's seat as Julie passed other businesses in town—a hardware store with little elves using the tools to make toys, a café with a window display of a gingerbread house that looked delicious, and the local grocery store with a donation bin outside wrapped in brightly colored wrapping paper and a sign that read *TOY DRIVE*. Each successive shop made her feel just a little more cheerful and less homesick for the city.

The animal shelter was less boisterously decorated than some of the other shops, but it, too, had lights strung up around all the windows and a humongous wreath on the door. There were plenty of spots, so she parked near the door.

When she came around the side of the truck to open the passenger's side door, the cold crept back into her numb feet. The cat turned in the carrier to glare at her through the bars, daring her to come close enough to get scratched.

"It's nothing personal," she told it, even though it was hard to sound genuine with the fresh scratches on her hands. "I don't live here. I can't keep you. I'm sure Myrtle will be able to find a better home for you."

The sound the cat made as Julie lifted the carrier was a cross between a hiss and a grumble. She slammed the truck door, locked it out of habit, and marched to the animal shelter door.

A bell chimed as she stepped inside. A mat on the

floor read Keep Your Paws Clean. She stamped the snow off her feet as she looked around. The front of the shelter was tiny, intimate. A long counter separated the front room, with only a single waiting chair, from the back, where the animals were presumably held. The open archway led to a warmly lit hallway with swags of evergreens along the top of the walls. It smelled Christmassy in here, probably due to the red candle burning low on the countertop. She didn't see or hear anyone, but Myrtle—or someone who worked for her—must be here.

"Hello?" Julie called.

A door opened and shut farther back in the shelter, and an old woman bustled into the hall. She moved slowly, but not in a way that indicated her health was in decline, and was still trim. She wore a red-and-green Christmas sweater with Rudolph in the center, complete with a red pom-pom for a nose. Julie wouldn't be caught dead in something like that, but it made her smile all the same.

"Myrtle?" She barely remembered Gram's friend —it had been so long since she'd visited Pinecone Falls. It didn't help that Myrtle had changed over the years as she grew into her late seventies, her hair turning a stately gray and her face and hands collecting wrinkles. Those wrinkles deepened around her mouth and eyes as she smiled.

"Why, Julie Green, it can't be. You look so grown up!"

I'm over thirty, Julie wanted to point out, but she didn't get the chance before she was pulled into a tight hug that left her breathless. She returned it more gently, even though it was clear the old woman was far from frail.

Myrtle pulled away, shorter than Julie by a head and beaming. "Your gram told me you'd be coming to town. So nice of you to think to stop in to see me."

Guilt wormed its way into Julie's stomach. She'd forgotten these small-town rules of etiquette where everyone knew everyone else, and one was expected to stop and say hello to people your grandparents knew and who you'd only seen years ago. She didn't want Myrtle to think she'd only come to drop off the cat, so she said, "You look good."

"Oh, pish," Myrtle said with a fling of her hand through the air. "I'm an old woman, and I know it. But you—you're in the prime of your life! And the spitting image of your gram when she was your age. Tell me, do you have a husband yet?"

Oh, yes. The other reason Julie didn't want to make the rounds in town. This question. She gritted her teeth through a smile. "I haven't had time, what with focusing on my career." A career that was floundering now that she had been laid off.

43

She changed the subject before Myrtle could tell her something like, *You don't have forever.* Dating hadn't been a big priority for her. Not to say that she hadn't dated—she had—but it had always been secondary to building herself the kind of life she wanted. That meant a steady job she liked, someday a house, and if she met the right person…

Julie cleared her throat and lifted the cat carrier. "Actually, while I'm here, I was hoping to leave this cat with you? I found him inside the inn."

Myrtle peered into the carrier and clucked at the cat. "You're a pretty one, aren't you?" Then the wrinkles at the corners of Myrtle's eyes deepened, this time with pity. "I'm sorry, though. The shelter is at full capacity."

Julie couldn't have heard right. She thrust the carrier toward the old woman. "Please, you have to take it. I don't live here, so I can't keep it. And it's mean."

Myrtle's mouth twitched. "It?" She opened the carrier and took out the cat. Of course, it acted perfectly affectionate, sinking into Myrtle's arms while shooting an angry glare at Julie. Myrtle stroked the cat a few times then held it up to look underneath before gently putting it back into the carrier. The cat never even attempted to scratch the older woman.

"It's not an 'it.' The cat is a *he*," Myrtle said. "And he doesn't seem mean at all."

Of course he didn't, not to Myrtle. Not loving the idea of having to deal with this murderous cat for nine more days, Julie begged, "Surely you can find room for one little cat. He seems well-fed, and his family is probably looking for him"

"Don't think so. Folks come here first thing a pet is missing. No one has come about a cat."

"It's a good idea to have him here for when they do come, though," Julie suggested.

Her stomach sank like a stone as Myrtle shook her head. "I can't. I just don't have the room. If I were to take him, I'd have to euthanize one of the cats already here."

Euthanize!

Instinctively, Julie jerked the cat carrier away from the old woman. The cat inside hissed his displeasure. She almost thrust it back, but the thought of handing him off just to be killed—or worse, for a perfectly *nice* cat to be killed in his place—made her cold. She might not like this cat, but she couldn't consign him to death. She wasn't a monster.

Weakly, Julie tried one last time. "Can't you put two cats in together?"

In this, Myrtle was firm. "No can do. Not all cats get along, and those are tight spaces to begin with.

They could injure each other! So, either you hold on to the cat until I have an opening, or I'll have to send for the vet to euthanize the cat that's been here the longest." After a moment's pause, Myrtle added, "That would be Gracie. Sweet thing. Missing most of her teeth but loves to cuddle."

It sounded to Julie like Myrtle was trying to get her to exchange this cat for a second one. She sighed. "I'll keep the cat. But please, you have to call me the second you have an opening or if her owners come in." She searched through her pockets until she found an old receipt that she could write her number down on. As she scrawled on the back of it using one of Myrtle's pens, the old woman babbled.

"I'm sure this guy is really a sweetheart deep down. He's probably just had a fright. And they respond to hostility, you know. If you approach him kindly, I'm sure you'll have no trouble. You could try visiting Pinecone Falls Pets to buy him a toy or two to keep him busy. That ought to calm him down."

If Julie was going to hold on to the cat until there was an opening at the shelter, she would need cat food. Even she knew that she couldn't keep feeding donuts to the darn thing. Resigned, she mustered some semblance of a smile and told Myrtle, "I'll do that." What else could she say?

. . .

SHE BROUGHT THE CARRIER BACK OUT TO THE TRUCK and deposited it onto the passenger seat again. This time, she leaned down to look the cat in the eye. "I guess we'll be hanging around together for a bit, after all. No more scratching, okay?"

He blinked at her, long and slow. Maybe she was imagining it, but she thought that for a split second, she detected a hint of trust in those eyes. Gratitude too.

Maybe this wouldn't be so bad after all.

❄

MYRTLE WAITED FOR THE DOOR TO SWING SHUT AFTER Julie before she let the smile spread across her face. Humming to herself, she returned to the back room. She passed cage after empty cage until she came to the few occupied with cats needing a home. She stopped in front of Gracie's cage. The Persian cat swished her fluffy tail and gave a small *mrrrow?*

"Not right now, sweetheart," Myrtle said, though she slipped her fingers in between the bars to scratch the cat between the ears. "I have to call Ida to let her know her granddaughter just came in. But don't you worry. I'll find a home for you."

Across from Gracie, a large tiger cat named

George gave a loud meow. Myrtle reached her hand in to pet him. "You, too, George."

She pulled her hand away and looked at all the cats in her care. "I'll find the perfect home for all of you. People don't know they need a cat until they're shown. Like Julie. I'm sure after she has this one for a few days, she'll be so in love, she'll have to keep him."

Myrtle fetched her phone and settled into the rocker in the corner to make the call. Ida picked up after two rings.

"Ida, it's Myrtle. You were right. Julie came in with the cat, just like you said she would."

Her friend sounded worried as she responded, "How was he? I was afraid, leaving him without anything there at the inn."

"He's fine. Used to be an old barn cat, though I think he's always been a house cat at heart. And before you ask, I told Julie the shelter was full up. She took the cat home with her."

If anything, Ida sounded relieved. "Good. She was always following that old cat of hers everywhere, and I know her apartment doesn't allow for pets. If she has this cat, it will be one more reason for her to stay in Pinecone Falls."

Myrtle rocked back and forth, content in her most favorite room in the whole world. "I'm sure you're right. She's not a city girl at heart. But are you sure this is what you want? I know you're a sneeze away from selling the property to Klaus Miller."

"I haven't finalized anything yet. It would be easy to back out of the sale, and just as easy to go through with it if Julie decides to go back to Boston after Christmas. But retirement doesn't suit me. I'd still be running that inn if I could do it on my own."

"Well, I hope she stays for your sake, then. It would be nice to have you back in town. The place isn't the same without you."

"Julie loves that inn like I do," Ida answered, her voice wistful. "I'm sure once she sees what Pinecone Falls can offer, she'll stay to help me run it. I suppose only time will tell... I only hope Klaus doesn't butt his head in and screw things up."

Myrtle shook her head. She wanted to say that that would never happen, but she and Ida had known Klaus a long time. "That man didn't use to be so grumpy. I suppose life has a way of beating you down."

"Not always. Life is what you make of it, and we're going to make the best of it. Julie too."

Myrtle smiled. "I hope you're right."

CHAPTER 6

$\mathcal{P}$inecone Falls Pets didn't have a sign on the door stating not to bring in a potentially murderous cat in a carrier, so Julie carried her temporary companion with her into the shop. The bell attached to the door jingled, but the store was suspiciously quiet. Julie glanced from side to side, taking in the aisles of pet food and toys—no pets themselves appeared to be sold in store. The door shut behind her, cutting off the stream of cold winter air.

No one else was in the shop. The counter to the right was empty, fitted with one of those new registers that worked off of a tablet instead of the clunky registers still found in most big-box retail stores. For a second, Julie wondered whether it was meant to be a self-serve option, but if so, who was to stop people from just taking what they wanted and walking out the door? No, the tablet was facing in the wrong direction. Someone was definitely meant to be behind it. Maybe they'd gone to the washroom or something.

Julie wasn't used to this kind of solitude while shopping. Even the small boutiques in downtown Boston always had employees ready to help—or watch—customers, a few of which were always in the store. Julie couldn't remember the last time she'd been in a store by herself. Even shopping after midnight at a twenty-four-hour grocery store, being the only customer wasn't a guarantee.

Shaking off her unease at the quiet, she set the cat carrier on top of the counter and started wandering the aisles for cat food. The aisles were neatly labeled by animal, so it wasn't difficult to find. In the back of one aisle, she crouched down and crunched some numbers in her head to try to decide which of these brands was the best deal. She didn't want to buy something that was only marginally better than powdered donuts. But she wasn't planning on keeping this cat, so she didn't want to invest in the expensive stuff either. In the end, she grabbed five cans of varying flavors. The cat would be gone long before then, she hoped.

"Well. You couldn't have come into the store by yourself."

Something about the woman's voice tickled at Julie's ears. Raising her free hand, she waved and straightened. "Sorry, he's with me. I just need to pick up a few things to tide him over for a few days."

"Julie?"

Julie tore her gaze away from the cat food display and toward the front of the store, where a petite woman in jeans and a T-shirt with a paw print had stopped in front of the counter. She had pulled her brown hair into a ponytail, but it was so curly, it looked more like a poof at the back of her head. Julie recognized her immediately.

"Ivy? My goodness, you're still here? It's been forever!" Memories of childhood escapades with Ivy rushed in. They'd been inseparable when Julie would visit Gram. She didn't see Ivy the rest of the year, but every time she came to visit, they picked up the friendship as if no time had passed. But Julie had "outgrown" visiting Gram before high school and hadn't seen Ivy since. She chased away a pang of guilt at not keeping in touch.

The brunette rolled her eyes and propped her hands on both hips. "Tell me about it. You shouldn't be such a stranger! And yes, I still live here. Well, I live here again. I left for college and came back. I own the store, actually."

"Wow." Julie glanced around the store with new

eyes. As a kid, Ivy had always loved pets, so she shouldn't be surprised. The store looked to be thriving and had Ivy's personal touches. Like the pet pictures all around the perimeter, which showed happy dogs, cats, birds, guinea pigs, and even a fish. Each image had a little name tag on the frame. Probably Ivy's own pets or maybe those of customers. Either way, it gave Julie a homey feeling.

Ivy was a part of the community, as integral here as Gram had been back in the day. In a way, Julie felt a little envious. She approached the counter and stacked the cat food cans next to the carrier. "This is a really nice store."

Ivy beamed. "Thank you. And what about you? What have you been doing?"

"Uh…" Julie did not want to admit that she was between jobs. "I'm a freelance writer. Nonfiction, mainly for magazines. But I'm here helping Gram put on one last Christmas Eve party up at the inn."

If anything, Ivy's grin turned even wider. "I remember the inn from back in the day. I was just getting the shop up and running when Ida retired. How is she?"

Sick. Julie didn't want to say that either. She shrugged. "Same as ever, I guess. I can tell she misses the inn, though."

"Well, it was her home for the past, what, seventy years?"

Gram had inherited the inn from her parents. "Longer than that, probably."

Ivy shook her head. "You can't blame her for not wanting to let it go." She leaned against the counter, her expression turning impish. "So, am I invited to this party?"

"Of course! If I'd known you were still in town, I would have gotten in touch somehow." It really had been too long. More images of the simple pleasures Julie and Ivy had enjoyed as kids surfaced. Looking for turtles in the creek, catching fireflies, and running through the forest together, along with a much more annoying boy named—

"Nolan Miller is back in town too."

Julie couldn't help but roll her eyes. "Oh, goody."

"He's not a little boy anymore. All grown up and *very* cute."

"Right." Julie flicked a lock of her hair out of her eyes. "Then why aren't you dating him?"

Ivy waggled her ring finger in the air between them to show off her rings. "I'm happily married. But I don't see a ring on *your* finger…"

Julie turned away. "I need kitty litter."

The one downside to there being no other customers in the store was that Ivy felt free to tag along behind her—just like Nolan had done, once upon a time.

In a singsong voice, Ivy said, "That isn't a no."

"Trust me. It doesn't matter how cute he's gotten. It's a no." She reached the cat litter and dragged out a container that looked like it would provide more than she would need. Her back still turned on her old friend, she dug around for a litter box.

Ivy handed her the scoop with a teasing smirk. "I'm telling you, he's grown up. You can't judge him for things he did while he was an annoying preteen."

Oh yes, Julie could. But even if she didn't, she wasn't in Pinecone Falls to find some kind of relationship. She didn't have *time* to find a relationship. And there was no way she was up for a fling, especially not with Nolan Miller. "I'm only here for the party. Then I'm going back to Boston."

Ivy propped her hands on her hips. "Right." That one word was laden with disbelief. "Then why did you get a cat if you're not staying?"

Julie groaned. She pressed the heels of her hands to her eyes and nearly poked herself with the litter scoop. "I did not *get* a cat. The cat came unbidden, like an ant infestation."

"You don't have to sound so thrilled about it. I thought you liked cats. Didn't you use to have one as a kid?"

Julie sighed, memories of Whiskers producing an unwanted longing in her chest. "I *do* like cats. I just don't like *this* cat. I found him in the inn, and he's been trouble ever since. But apparently, the animal shelter is full up right now, so I have to keep him until Myrtle has an opening." She started to heft the heavy container of litter, only to get a brilliant idea. Brimming with hope, she asked, "I don't suppose you'd like a cat?"

Ivy shook her head. "Josh is allergic. My husband," she clarified.

Julie's shoulders slumped in defeat. "Well, it was worth a shot."

Owning and working in a pet shop must have added some muscle to Ivy's curvy physique, because she lifted the litter as if it weighed nothing, leaving Julie to take the rest. As they returned to the register, Julie recalled Myrtle's advice and grabbed a toy mouse off one of the racks at random.

"I refuse to believe he's trouble," Ivy cooed as she reached the counter. She bent to peer into the carrier. "He looks like a sweetheart."

Of course, the cat didn't hiss at *her*.

"What's his name?" Ivy asked as she straightened. She turned the tablet toward her to begin ringing up the order.

"He doesn't have one. And I'm *not* giving him one. I'm not keeping him because——"

"You're only here for a few days. Right." As Julie fished out her credit card to pay, Ivy bagged the items and added one of her business cards. She scrawled a number on the back. "My cell. We should get together while you're in town."

Julie relaxed. "Actually, that would be nice."

Ivy tapped a button on the screen and asked, "Do you want a paper receipt?"

"No, thanks."

Without being asked, Ivy gathered up the litter and one of the bags and followed Julie out of the store to her waiting truck. Fortunately, she'd parked it on the street within eyesight of Pinecone Falls Pets. After they'd loaded up the truck with Julie's purchases and the unwanted cat, Ivy patted the carrier and shut the passenger door.

"I think he'll win you over," she said cheerily.

"Don't hold your breath."

With mock innocence, the shorter woman—who must be freezing without a coat—said, "Aren't you going to ask which *he* I'm talking about, Nolan or the cat?"

Julie turned away without dignifying that with an answer. "I have groceries to buy. I'll text you."

Ivy's laugh followed her into the truck.

CHAPTER 7

"Here we are," Julie muttered under her breath as she parked the truck in front of the Cozy Holly Inn. "Home sweet home." She shut off the engine and turned to the cat carrier. It was facing the wrong direction for her to see inside, but tufts of white fur showed through the gaps in the plastic.

Julie had about a hundred things to carry inside, but first, she let the cat free into the house. He bolted out of sight. She could just imagine what new mess he was leaving for her somewhere inside the old house. Well, the joke was on him. She hadn't even started cleaning up yet, so it was all the same to her.

The cat litter came out next, and she even found a spot for it in the bathroom and poured a healthy amount into the pan before returning for the bags of food—both for the cat and for herself. Her feet were blocks of ice by this point in her suede boots, and she didn't want to have to make yet another trip, so she just scooped it all into one gigantic armload.

At the door, she regretted that decision. The wind had swept a drift of snow onto the porch, so she didn't want to set the bags of food and cleaning supplies down in the snow. She juggled them instead, the fingers of her left hand aching with the weight as she quickly reached for the doorknob with her mostly free hand.

The door creaked open. A streak of white raced into the snow. Julie swore under her breath.

"Darn it!" She shoved the bags into the inn, shut the door, and tramped down the steps. "I could let you freeze, you know." The cat blended in with the snow so perfectly that she could barely see it in the drifts.

She heard a loud bark. Chills raced down her spine. That couldn't be good. Despite the heels on her boots, she lunged into the snow. It came up to her knees and somehow found gaps between her jeans and boots she hadn't realized were there. Now losing feeling in her toes *and* her ankles, she gritted her teeth and pushed forward.

She didn't have far to go. A large dog, as white and fluffy as the cat, planted its paws on an evergreen tree trunk. It was nearly as tall as her while standing! She froze, for a moment afraid it was a wolf or something and would turn on her next.

Thankfully the dog was wearing a bright-red collar, meaning that someone owned it. Meaning it was tame. Probably.

She advanced on the dog and swatted the air with her hands. "Shoo. Shoo, you! You shouldn't be here."

The barks paused. The dog sat on its haunches and turned its head, ears perked up into wide triangles over its fluffy face as it surveyed Julie. *Don't show fear.* Dogs could smell it on a person, couldn't they?

Except… the dog looked anything but vicious. It looked kind of sweet with its wagging tail and curious eyes that darted from Julie to the tree.

Although Julie was leery of taking her eyes off the unchaperoned dog, she glanced quickly up at the branches of the tree. Yes, there was the cat. Great. One more disaster to add to her morning.

She swatted her hands toward the dog again. "Shoo. I'll never get him down with you here."

The dog, probably a husky of some kind despite the lack of the usual gray coloring, didn't move an inch. It also didn't seem to be the least bit concerned to be sitting in a giant pile of snow.

Julie mumbled under her breath as she sidled closer to the tree. The dog stood. She held out her hands. "No. Stay right there. Don't come any closer."

Above her, on a branch just out of reach, the cat watched with narrowed eyes. Clearly, he wasn't inclined to be any help.

Maybe she should go back in the house and wait for the dog to leave? She couldn't do that. The cat might freeze, or what if he came down and the dog got him?

"Snowball?"

The dog perked up its ears at the sound of the man's voice. It turned in a circle, excited, before bounding away. Thank goodness. Maybe now Julie had a chance to rescue the wayward cat. She braced the toe of her boot against the rough bark of the tree trunk, made slippery by the snow, and reached overhead to grip the sturdiest-looking branch.

Behind her, a dog barked. She yelped, lost her grip, and tumbled onto her butt in the snow.

Great. Just great. This was the cherry on her day.

"Snowball, come here."

Though, come to think of it, Snowball was an adorable name for a dog. Julie looked up through the wisps of blond hair falling in front of her face at the man who had emerged from the trees. He wore solid snow boots, the kind that laced up to the calf, well-worn jeans, and a heavy brown coat. That coat fit over broad shoulders and up to a face that made her thoughts stop in their tracks.

No. It couldn't be.

Nolan Miller extended a gloved hand. "Sorry about that. She tends to get overly enthusiastic when she meets new people."

Numbly, Julie put her hand in his and let him pull her to her feet. Although his gloves weren't covered in snow, the leather was cold to the touch. His brown eyes were warm as he smiled at her encouragingly, displaying a slight gap in his teeth that solidified her suspicions. Nolan Miller had grown into his front teeth, the gap making him look more boyish than awkward. It was definitely him.

His eyes narrowed. "Wait. Julie Green? Is that you?"

"Yep. Nolan Miller?"

"Yes. Good to see you. Gosh, it's been a long time." He looked down at her bare hands. "Did you lose your gloves?"

Nolan was looking around at the snow and the imprint Julie had made in it when she'd fallen. She shook her head. "I left them inside. I didn't plan to be out long."

He dropped his gaze to her feet. "Those boots really aren't made for snow country. If you're planning on traipsing around out here, you should get yourself some Sorel boots, or maybe North Face. The store in town sells them. Looks like you might need a warmer coat too."

Great, unsolicited advice. Apparently, Nolan hadn't changed that much in the intervening years, after all.

Julie crossed her arms. She was freezing, from her cheeks to the soles of her feet. "Thanks for the fashion tips. I wouldn't even be out here if your dog hadn't chased the cat up the tree." She pointed overhead.

Nolan tipped his head back and looked up at the cat. "Well, I haven't seen you around here."

Julie didn't know whether he was talking to her or the cat. "Do you know all the animals that hang around in these woods?"

He tilted his head to turn his smile on her. "Pretty much. I live at the lodge full time now, helping my father and grandfather out," he said, pointing down a deer trail cutting between the trees. Through the gap, she could just make out the roof of a stone building impressive enough to look like a castle from this distance. "Snowball and I spend a lot of time walking in the woods."

She vaguely remembered Nolan only visited in summers back when they were kids. Truth was she'd hardly paid much attention to him back then. And she doubted she would now either.

"There are bobcats roaming the area. You should keep your cat inside," he said.

More annoying advice.

He stood there examining the branches leading up to the cat perched out of reach over his head as if formulating a plan to get him down.

"If you'll take your dog someplace else, I'm sure I can get the cat down myself."

The dog in question calmly lumbered between her and Nolan and sat patiently on its rump. It looked up at Julie with soft brown eyes.

"I assume Snowball chased him up there? If so, I should fix the problem, shouldn't I?"

Was Nolan always this unshakably cheerful? He flashed her another smile before he gripped two of the branches and easily started to climb up.

"Besides, you haven't been here in what, a decade? I bet you've lost your knack for tree climbing."

It was a knack she'd never really had to begin with. Probably one of the reasons why she'd acclimated so well to city life.

When he was almost within arm's reach, he stretched out a hand to the cat. The cat looked at it like he was offering a lemon. Almost curious enough to smell him, but with a disdain clear in every line of his feline body.

"What's his name? Maybe he'll be friendlier if I call him."

"He doesn't have one."

Nolan pulled his arm back and gripped a tree branch loosely as he turned to look down at her. His feet were only near her shoulder height, and he seemed comfortable, nestled between the pine boughs.

"He doesn't have one?"

"He's not my cat. I found him in the house, and the animal shelter is full up. He'll only be here until they get an opening."

Shaking his head, Nolan turned back to the tree and climbed another branch to get a more secure spot closer to the cat. Despite his attempts at cajoling, the cat didn't seem inclined to leap into his arms. At least his dog didn't bark and make things worse, but the giant dog had decided to circle back and forth beneath the tree with a loopy grin on her face.

The cat stretched his neck, sniffing at Nolan, and in one graceful move, he swooped the ball of fur into his arms. "Gotcha."

Nolan climbed down as easily as he had gone up. When he reached the lowest branch, the cat cradled to his chest with one hand, the cat decided that he had had enough. With a wild yowl, he scratched at Nolan, launched himself from his arms, and raced through the snow toward the inn's front porch.

"Snowball, stay!" Nolan commanded.

The dog, coiling to run after, instead sat at the base of the tree and gave a dejected sigh.

Nolan hopped down the last couple feet from the tree and examined a rip in his glove.

"See? He's a monster."

Nolan grunted. "He still deserves a name."

When he looked up, their eyes caught. In the shadow of the tree, his were so dark, they were almost black. Captivating. Julie took a step back, giving herself a mental shake.

"Well, thanks for the rescue. I'd better go let him inside."

She'd taken two steps toward the house when Nolan called after her. "What brings you here, anyway?"

Her shoulders tensed, and she turned. His hand was on the ruff of his dog's neck, gently holding her back. His expression was unreadable.

Julie pointed to the house. "It's my family inn."

"I know, but your grandmother is selling to us, and it's been closed for years, so I just wondered."

Her eyebrows winged up under the cover of her bangs. Why was he asking so many questions? Was it just curiosity, or was he looking out for the new family investment?

"We're throwing one last Christmas Eve party before it's gone."

Nolan's gaze drifted to the house, frown lines tugging between his brows. "Seems like a lot of work to get it fixed up for one party."

He had a point. "We're not renovating, just a quick spruce up and then the party. Gram wants to since it will be the last one." Saying it out loud made her feel sad.

"Right. I guess I'll leave you it, then." His voice was stiff but polite. "Keep an eye out for bobcats."

She turned and headed through the snow. The inn, though it looked in a state of disrepair, softened her prickly mood. She had so many fond memories of this place.

Somehow, she got the feeling that the Millers were not going to take care of it like Gram had. That thought, more than anything else, made her sad to see it go.

CHAPTER 8

Snowball bobbed and weaved among the stark brown trees, almost blending in with the heaps of snow beneath them. Her levity helped to ease some of the tension Nolan had been carrying since rescuing the cat. He was usually a pretty laid-back guy, but something about seeing Julie again had brought back old memories.

He might not have recognized her, but the grown-up Julie looked a lot like her grandmother. He remembered playing as kids, looking for frogs in the pond, climbing trees—Julie had never been good at that, so it was probably a good thing she hadn't tried to rescue that cat. He didn't remember much of her beyond that and the sweep of freckles along her nose. Her freckles hadn't been so prominent today, either because of the season or because she hid them under makeup now. Strangely, he found that he missed them.

It wasn't that she didn't look lovely without them —she did—but the faint dusting along her cheeks and nose, all but covered by the color brought on by the cold, made her seem more remote. Less approachable. Maybe she liked it that way. It was none of his business, really. He shouldn't even be thinking about her attractiveness. Not because she was the enemy or something ridiculous like that, but because Nolan had no time to find a woman attractive.

He didn't date. It wasn't that he avoided it; it was that he couldn't spare the time away from the inn and his family. His mother had been the glue tying them all together, and even if Nolan fit badly in her place, if he suddenly had more important things to do elsewhere, he didn't want to think of what would happen to Gramps and his dad.

Hence, no dating. No finding women attractive.

No Julie.

Absorbed in his thoughts, Nolan didn't notice when the trees along the deer path thinned and the lodge with the stables nestled alongside came into view. Snowball launched from between the last of the trees and caught him unawares. She hit him like a freight train, and he flew backward into the snow.

For a moment, he sat there, staring up at the overcast sky, wondering what the heck had happened. Then the dog bounced into view, happily licking his face. It was cold enough out here that he could feel her wet kisses start to freeze on his skin. He nudged her away with a laugh.

"Snowball, enough."

Her tongue lolling, she sat in the snowbank next to him. When Nolan extricated himself, she leaned down, her rump high, her tail thrashing the air. She wanted to play. Nolan packed together a tight snowball and let it fly. She raced after it, up to her shoulders in snow as she pushed through the drifts along the path. When she couldn't find the snowball, she ran in circles before realizing she had been tricked.

Nolan laughed again, feeling years of weight lift from his shoulders. It didn't matter that he didn't have time for romance. Snowball was all he needed.

She barreled through the snow again toward him. This time, he caught her in midair, bracing himself. She wiggled free and dropped the short distance to the ground. Still full of energy, she chased her tail in a manic circle.

"Settle down, girl."

She sat. He kneeled in front of her, taking some time to comb the clumps of snow and ice from her fur. She vibrated with energy but remained still for his attentions.

"Good girl. Can't have you running amok in the lodge, now can we?"

She cracked a canine smile.

As he brushed away the worst of the snow, he thought about Julie. Not about how pretty she was, with her blond hair cut to her chin and the coat and jeans that hugged her figure. No, about what she'd said.

"Ida Green is selling the property to us. So why did she send her granddaughter to throw a party? That sounds more like someone who's having second thoughts and wants to announce a grand reopening."

Snowball tilted her head. She obviously didn't see the problem.

Nolan did. Gramps had his heart set on expanding their property to include the old house.

Nolan sighed. "I just don't want to see Gramps disappointed. He's been through enough." First, with his wife passing. Then, with his daughter. After Gram had passed, Nolan's mom had been the life of the lodge, even on the days when the chemo had her bedridden. Nolan didn't have her bubbly personality.

"I miss her," he whispered.

Snowball licked his chin.

Right. If he stayed out here, his face was going to freeze. He forced himself to stand. "Come on, girl. Let's go home."

The attention had calmed her down enough that she trotted at his side rather than bounding through the snow and undoing all their hard work. As they passed the stables, one of the horses whinnied. Snowball stopped in her tracks, ears perked to attention.

"All right," Nolan conceded. "But only for a minute."

When he changed course to step toward the stables, Snowball pranced ahead of him. A word of caution slowed her at the entrance.

"Be good," he warned. The very last thing he wanted was for his dog to rile the horses.

Fortunately, they were used to Snowball coming and going, more so in the summer, and when Nolan pulled open the sliding door to admit them, the nearest horses gave no more than disdainful snorts. Snowball took their condescension in stride and trotted up to a gelding who had his nose lowered outside his stall box. They sniffed each other, a courtesy.

Nolan crossed to his mare, a bay with a white blaze on her face, and stroked her between the eyes. "Hi there, Dolly."

She softly lipped at his gloves.

"Sorry, I don't have any treats for you right now. I'll come back later."

He continued to stroke the mare, watching as

Snowball pranced from stall to stall to greet each of her reluctant friends. Dolly found the rip in his glove and gave it a tug. He affectionately patted her on the nose as he pulled that glove away before she could do more damage to it. It was only a small rip; he might be able to sew it himself, a skill passed down from his mom.

The stables consisted only of a half dozen stalls, and Snowball found her way to the end of them quickly. Instead of crossing the aisle to greet the horses on the other side, she started to sniff the tarp-covered shape in the back.

Nolan's levity disappeared like smoke.

"That's enough, Snowball. Come on."

He turned without looking to see whether she obeyed him. Even he didn't want to look at that tarp-covered shape and the memories held beneath. Although he was glad that Gramps had kept on the horses when they'd stopped offering sleigh rides to their patrons, he didn't know why he or Stan hadn't sold the sleigh. They had destroyed every other Christmas memory.

At the door, he stared at the tarp for a minute, easily picturing the sleek, red-painted sleigh beneath. His mom had adored it, pushing herself well beyond what she should have endured in her condition just to find herself on the padded bench, swathed in blankets and watching the snow-covered fields pass by.

Snowball joined him at the door, and he shut it, cutting off the sight.

"It's not as though we'll ever use it again." He took one last look at the tarp, picturing the sleigh with his mother and her last ride the day before she passed. The memory caused his eyes to burn, and he quickly pulled the doors shut and headed back to the lodge.

❄

His father found him inside, cozy in a knit sweater and reviewing the bookings on his laptop in front of the fire in the main room.

"You look like someone just set your dog on fire."

Nolan shook himself. On instinct, he looked down at his feet, where Snowball had curled herself within the halo of the grate. She opened her eyes but didn't move from the comfortable spot.

"Just working," Nolan muttered, as much to himself as to his dad. But he shut the computer.

Stan wasn't the man Nolan remembered growing up. It wasn't that his hairline had receded, or he'd put on weight around his middle—both true. It was the way he held himself, shoulders hunched as if trying to ward away conversation before it even started. But even *he* was more talkative than Gramps.

"I saw Julie Green today."

Stan scowled. "Ida's granddaughter?"

Nolan nodded.

"What's she doing here?"

"She said she was here to throw one last Christmas Eve party before the property is sold."

It shouldn't have come as a surprise to Nolan to see his father's expression darken. It always did at the mention of Christmas, at the reminder of his loss. It was why they didn't have stockings along the fireplace or Christmas photos lining the top or a tree in the space in front of the wide window. After three years, Nolan had gotten used to the sparseness of the season, but the guests continued to ask after decorations, especially those who had visited during a Christmas before Mary had died.

Stan had said they were too much bother. All the trouble of putting up all those decorations only to take them down again in a couple weeks. But Nolan knew the real reason. It was the painful reminder of losing his wife that stopped them from putting up reminders of the Christmas season.

"That's a terrible idea."

"Because the inn has been empty for years or because of the holiday?" Nolan felt guilty as soon as the words were out of his mouth. He was usually sympathetic to his father's grief, but he was starting to think his hatred of the holiday was unhealthy. What could he do to snap his dad out of it? Nolan couldn't help but feel some fond memories of past Christmases with his mom would help, but Stan was resistant to any mention of it.

His father pinned him with a glare. "Both." He turned and left the room.

Snowball raised her chin onto Nolan's knee, and he petted her absently. There had to be some way to help his father out of his sadness, but Nolan had no idea what it was.

❄

THE WHITE CAT HAD CLAIMED GRAM'S FAVORITE chair.

Julie didn't mind, seeing as she had never had the gall to sit in that chair unless she was sitting in Gram's lap. She took a spot on the couch instead. It sank beneath her weight, the springs groaning, but she tried not to take that personally. It was an old couch. She pulled out her phone and opened an app to take notes.

"All right. Nine days left before the party. Let's see what I have to do."

The cat, helpfully, did not answer. His eyes were closed, and his feet were tucked beneath his chest in a way that made him look like a fluffy loaf of bread.

Julie looked at the trail of dust her footsteps had left through the room. "Cleaning. That should probably be first on the list. I'll have to do the downstairs rooms and the bathrooms. Probably not all the bedrooms." Though if she got bored, it would be something to occupy her. She'd already learned that the data connection on her phone was not good enough to stream video.

"I have to speak to the caterer."

The cat blinked open one curious eye.

"Not for you," she muttered. "You know where your food cans are."

He was quick on the uptake, she'd give him that. Once she'd fed him once and put away the rest of the cans, he'd been meowing at the cabinet ever since. It was a miracle he wasn't in there now.

"I have a number for that somewhere…" She found the note she'd made and called the caterer before she forgot. She'd already talked to the woman about the party, but she had wanted to come over and see the kitchen to make sure it would be adequate for heating up food and serving. She made a quick appointment for the next afternoon and crossed it off the list she'd made earlier on the back of an old envelope she'd found in a drawer.

"Next we need to locate some cleaning supplies and get this place spiffed up." Julie made a check mark next to that item, indicating it was in progress. "There. Doesn't that make us feel productive?"

The cat squinted at her, with the other eye this time.

She scowled. "I could do without your judgment, cat."

He shut his eye.

Julie harrumphed and went back to her to-do list. "What else? I'll have to decorate, but that can only be done after the cleaning." She glanced at the next item. "I know this place needs a couple of repairs too. I have a number for a repair guy in town…"

She was flipping through the notes on her phone when the cat jumped off of Gram's chair and trotted away, tail held high.

"Cat! Cat—hey, where are you going?"

She really had to stop calling him "cat." For one thing, it felt wrong. For another, it wasn't as though the cat ever responded to it. Afraid that the mischievous animal would do more damage to the inn while her back was turned, Julie hopped to her feet and followed.

She reached the kitchen just as the cat jumped on

the counter and pawed ineffectually at the cupboard. He looked at her and mewled.

"No. I've already fed you today. Which is pretty much as much as I've fed myself." Maybe she should add "eat supper" to the to-do list. Not that she was the greatest cook. When she'd picked up the cleaning supplies, she'd thrown a couple boxes of mac and cheese into the shopping cart, along with the milk and butter to make it. That would have to be good enough.

With one hand, she reached out to lift the cat from the counter and deposit him on the floor.

Hiss! He swatted out, and Julie jumped back.

"Okay, fine. I get it. No picking up. And you wonder why I'm not feeding you again, Grouchy."

She found the mouse toy she'd bought for him and tossed it. He pounced, content to be distracted for the moment.

Although she still needed to take a good look at the outside of the house and decide which repairs she was going to have done—if the Millers were buying the property as is, it seemed a waste to do them at all —she capitalized on the decent cell phone signal in the kitchen and called the number of the first repair guy Gram had given her. Bob Ryder.

Bob sounded about as old as Gram, but he was more than willing to come out the next day and fix up a few odds and ends. So that was one more thing checked off her list.

She looked at the floor of the kitchen and sighed. Now, for the hard part.

Where had she put the mop?

ornings in Pinecone Falls were little pieces of magic, especially in winter. Nolan had always been something of a morning person, eager to roll out of bed and start his day. When he'd moved to Barrington Lodge, that day had always started with tending the horses, and it was perhaps his favorite way of waking up. When they didn't try to kick him, at least.

After brushing and turning out the horses—or, in this case, shuffling them around so he could muck out their stalls—he and Snowball were left with time to roam. Since Snowball liked snow even better than she liked the horses, it was time that Nolan took for granted.

And yes, maybe he should have paid more attention to where his steps were taking him, instead of soaking in the idyllic scene of snow-capped evergreens and the occasional cardinal or blue jay. There were deer in these woods, too, but they were shy. With Snowball by his side, he rarely ever saw the animals, but he did see their tracks. He didn't mind, though. This time, this quiet morning before he had to involve himself with the running of the inn, was only for him and Snowball.

When the roof of the Cozy Holly Inn peeked through the trees, he paused in his step. When had he stepped over the property line?

"Snowball?"

She didn't respond to his soft call but loped on ahead. Nolan picked up his pace. Maybe he could stop her from chasing any more wayward cats if he hurried.

Ahead, Snowball gave a soft *wuff*. It was her indoor voice, the only voice he let her use around the horses. The big dog was standing hip-deep in snow, tail wagging vigorously as she beheld the woman staring at the back of the inn with crossed arms and narrowed eyes. Maybe she sensed that Julie was skittish. Snowball could be surprisingly astute that way.

Julie pulled from whatever trance she'd been in, looked around, and yelped when she saw how close the dog was—the wrong end of a pounce away. The yelp, Snowball took as an invitation to play. She coiled in preparation for jumping.

"Snowball!"

Too late.

Julie managed to avoid one hundred pounds of dog knocking her back into the snow but lost her balance. She scrabbled for the nearest handhold—the railing of that rickety, wraparound porch. The wood creaked. It held.

Nolan was already halfway across the lawn before he registered that she was in no danger. She saw him coming and released her death grip on the railing, regaining her balance and recrossing her arms.

Her hair was in that perfect bob, the blond highlights catching the sunlight reflecting off the glittering white snow. She wore those good-for-nothing boots again. And today, she didn't even have on her coat, only a cable-knit sweater that went up to her chin. Did this woman have any sense at all? Or did she only care for fashion—even if it meant frostbite?

Nolan hadn't had any coffee yet, so of course, the first thing that came out of his mouth was, "Where's your coat?"

She stared at him, blinking owlishly. "Where's my *what?*"

"Your coat." He'd already put his foot in his mouth. He couldn't take it back now.

"What are you, my dad?"

"Uh, no." He forced himself not to sweep his gaze over the figure that sweater clung to intimately. "Definitely not."

Snowball barked, interrupting the awkward moment.

He smiled, even though it felt strained. "Come here, girl."

"Do you ever put that dog on a leash?"

Julie was hugging herself so tightly, her sweater would probably leave an imprint on her skin.

Nolan frowned. "Are you afraid of dogs?"

"What? No. She just came out of nowhere and she's... *big*."

When Nolan held out his hand, Snowball came to sit at his feet. He didn't even have to call her name; she knew him that well. He scratched her behind the ears. "She's playful, but she'd never intentionally hurt you."

The arms around her middle eased, but the tightness of her mouth didn't. "Are you here for a reason?"

He tried not to take the bite in her voice personally. "Just out for a walk."

"Here?" She gestured to the yard, and he guessed she was wondering why he was on her property. He couldn't blame her, really.

"We were walking in the woods, and Snowball came running over here, so I came to find her," he said.

"Oh." She shivered.

He cleared his throat, trying to find some way to turn this from awkward to neighborly.

With a smile that he hoped didn't look as forced as it felt, he teased, "Must be warm in the city, or have you forgotten how cold it is in Pinecone Falls?"

"I only came out here for a minute to look at the porch railing and make sure it's safe." Her lips turned up in a shadow of a smile. "I guess I did forget how cold it can get, though."

Nolan eyed the railing. "Anything I can help with?"

Uncertainty flickered in her eyes. She wasn't wearing makeup this morning, and he could see all her freckles she'd had hidden the day before. They made her look softer, more approachable.

"No, thanks. I can handle it."

"Of course."

"Well, I have things to do inside. Try to keep a handle on your dog. She scares the cat," she said as she retreated up the steps.

He would have been more offended if she hadn't reached out almost aimlessly to touch Snowball's fur as she passed. He bit back a smile as he ushered

Snowball back toward home. Julie liked dogs more than she let on.

Which was good. He didn't know whether he could like someone who didn't like his dog.

And for the sake of the sale going smoothly, it was better he didn't add more friction between their families. At least, that was what he told himself.

CHAPTER 10

*I*t was probably a good thing that the cat appeared to dislike Julie. He made a point to leave the room or hide whenever Julie tried to engage him. She told herself that this was best, so she wouldn't get attached. Still, one little snuggle, or at least letting her pet his soft fur, wouldn't be too bad, would it?

"I'm not a monster," she told the cat.

He didn't answer. He was hiding underneath Gramps's rocker, a precarious place to be in the best of times, especially since his long fluffy tail kept swishing under one of the runners.

"You could get hurt."

The cat didn't seem to believe her.

She sighed, rubbing her hands together to get

them warm and remembering Nolan's critique of her outerwear.

"I haven't forgotten the winters in Vermont," she muttered under her breath. She paced the living room, waiting for the sound of a car. Bob would be here any minute, and she was anxious to get him started and knock another task off the list.

The cat tensed at the sound of what she was waiting for. It was muffled, the snow not being as crunchy as it might have been, but the unmistakable rumble of a truck engine hailed someone's arrival. She hurried to the door to meet Bob.

Bob Ryder looked exactly as he'd sounded on the phone. He was about the same age as her grandmother but robust. He had a bit of a potbelly half hidden by the heavy plaid jacket he wore. He carried with him a box of tools in his gloved hand. His truck was a much older model than the one Julie had rented, and sitting next to the rental in front of the inn, it looked its age.

Bob smiled as he saw her. He took the stairs at a careful pace, holding on to the railing once he tested his weight on it. It wiggled a bit, causing him to mutter under his breath. Probably one more thing to fix. Hopefully just a loose screw and not the wood itself.

When he reached her, he put the toolbox down

on the porch she'd swept clean of snow this morning and offered his hand. She took it. He had a firm handshake, despite his years.

"I can't say I ever thought to see you in Pinecone Falls again."

Self-consciously, she held out her hands. "Well, here I am."

"That you are. And you look just like your gram too. I can't believe so much time has passed." He gave a hearty sigh then stamped his feet. "Well, why don't you show me what needs doing."

Before they went inside, Julie showed him the spindle on the railing she wanted replaced—it was front and center and, having been broken by good-ness-knew-what, could be a danger risk to an unsus-pecting guest. Inside, she started to lead him to the kitchen, where one of the cabinets was falling off the hinges—not the one in which she kept the cat food, much to the cat's dismay.

Bob stopped short in the living room. The cat had vacated his spot beneath the rocker, and without that sign of life, it looked quiet and lonely. Everything was clean—Julie had scrubbed the floor to within an inch of its life—but without Gram and Gramps and an assortment of guests there, it was only a room. Only empty furniture.

"My wife and I used to come to these parties

every year. Long before your time," he added with a chuckle. His eyes shining in the light coming in from the window, he gestured to the fireplace next to the rocker. "We used to take our picture in front of that fireplace, every year. She called it good luck."

"And was it?"

He looked at her, as though startled she was still here. She felt like she shouldn't be, like she was intruding on a private moment. But his expression was soft and a bit sad, not accusing. "Anything that made her happy was good luck if you ask me." He hesitated a moment then added, "She passed on a few years back. But Eloise… I still have these fond memories of her, of a place she loved. It's enough."

To her surprise, he caught her hand. She flexed her fingers but didn't pull away, even though she felt a bit awkward. The look in his eyes was too intense.

"Thank you," he said thickly. "For doing what Ida can't anymore. For making this party happen so I can remember her that way one more time."

Julie's throat felt thick with emotion. "You're welcome," she whispered back, and she tried for a smile too. She wasn't sure she succeeded.

He cleared his throat and pulled away. "Now what else do you want me to fix here?"

She led him to the kitchen, but as she did, she couldn't help but think of how she'd never been thanked for doing a job before. In the magazine world, there was always another deadline, never any recognition of having undertaken or achieved it.

It was… nice, to be thanked.

❄

As Julie left Bob in the kitchen and ventured to the attic to grab some of the decorations, his heart-felt appreciation for her organizing the party made her feel a little lighter.

Bob's gratitude had been raw and genuine. It made her feel soft and valued in a way that she had never felt before. She'd never realized that the party held precious memories for some, and it felt good to be able to bring those back.

There's no better feeling than helping someone. One of Gram's favorite sayings echoed in her head.

She still had the other floors to clean and rooms to prepare, but for now, she wanted to see the decorations, to see what she was working with. Maybe this party wasn't just some frivolous excuse to say goodbye to the inn. Maybe it touched people in ways Julie had never considered.

She was considering it now, as she carefully stepped down from the attic bearing the weight of a large box of decorations. She was almost at the bottom when she heard a yowl. She had stepped on something fluffy, a tail, and quickly moved off of it. The cat, rather than running away, jostled between her legs and up to the attic. Julie stumbled. The box came crashing to the ground, and it was only by clinging to the rickety banister that she didn't wind up next to it.

She glared up at the cat, who glared back. "Are you trying to kill me?"

He made no reply.

With her heart still beating frantically, Julie righted the box. There were breakable things in this one, ornaments and ceramic angels. She opened the lid, holding her breath. Everything was wrapped in yellowed newspaper, but what if that hadn't been enough to protect it? She peeked into the paper, one by one, and set each intact decoration aside. A clay reindeer she'd made when she was ten. A glass ornament marked with the year she'd been born. Other, older ones, too, angels with trumpets and harps that were so old the painting on their faces had worn off. Heirlooms, that Gram had from her own grandmother, and even older, passed down generation by generation. All intact, safe in their paper wadding.

Then she saw one angel wing peeking out of the wad of newspaper still in the bin. Julie forgot how to breathe. It was the tree topper. This one, too, had a face that was no more than a suggestion. The wings were gold, woven in a way that mimicked lace. The body was crystalline. Fearful, Julie unwrapped the angel with shaking hands.

It was in one piece. *Thank goodness.* She shut her eyes tight as she held the angel to her chest.

Mrrrow?

She opened her eyes. The cat was sitting on the last step now, more curious than sullen. His eyes were wide, but the pupils took up almost all of the blue, and his tail thrashed. He looked ready to pounce.

Julie turned her torso away, sheltering the tree topper. "Oh, no, you don't. These are priceless. They aren't toys."

The cat, as usual, ignored her.

But she managed to fend him away as she rewrapped the ornaments and replaced them in the box. She didn't try to lift the box again but sat with her back to the wall. She was feeling sentimental. She was remembering too many Christmases spent in this house, too many summers. She dug her phone out of her pocket and scrolled through her contacts until she found the one she'd added yesterday.

Ivy.

Before she thought better of it, she texted. She was never good at reaching out first, but she tried anyway. What could be the harm?

Julie: Hi. This is Julie.

She didn't expect a response right away. Leaning her head back against the wall, she reached out her hand to the cat and cooed, rustling her fingers.

He looked at her with disdain from his perch at the bottom of the stairs, just one step above her.

Her phone chirped. Julie checked the message.

Ivy: Hi! I'm so glad you texted. Want to do lunch?

Julie bit her lip as she texted back. She almost said yes instantly, but remembered that aside from Bob, she was also waiting on the caterer today.

Julie: I can't today. I have some party errands to finish up.

Ivy: Tomorrow?

Julie's answer was instant.

Julie: Yes.

She rested her head against the wall, this time with a smile. Her gaze wandered past the standoffish cat—she tried not to take it personally—to the box of ornaments. The tree topper, carefully wrapped, was on the top of the bundle now. When she was a kid, Gramps used to lift her to put that tree topper on the tree every year. When she got too big to lift, he'd put out the stepladder for her.

Which reminded her, she needed to find a tree. But first, she needed to check on Bob.

CHAPTER 11

*J*ulie reached the kitchen just as Bob was testing the hinges on the cabinet door. It swung easily open and shut without that jarring crunching sound she'd noticed, or the way it listed to one side. It was fixed.

"Next I'll do the spindle and the rail out front," Bob assured her, "but I wanted to let you know about something I noticed first."

His tone of voice made her stomach sink.

He opened the cabinet door to reveal the pipes beneath the sink. "You've got a leak in there." With the door open, not muffling the sound, she could hear the intermittent *drip, drip, drip.*

She peeked in to see the bottom of the cabinet was wet. She backed out and looked up at Bob. "Can you fix it?"

"I don't do plumbing, but Ned Wheatly does." Bob shut the door with care. "It's a good thing Ida had the water turned off while it was closed up. I'm sorry I didn't check under the cabinets when I turned it back on. It's not a huge deal, but you should call Ned to get that fixed as soon as you can. You'll have mold and who knows what else, otherwise."

Julie tried to keep her growing dismay out of her voice as she thumbed the name into the notes on her phone. "That wouldn't be good. I hope Ned can come out soon."

"Don't you worry. He knew Ida. I'm sure he'll be delighted to run on over and fix this as soon as he can."

After digging around in his pockets, Bob found an old receipt and a pen. He scrawled a number on the back of the receipt and held it out to her.

Julie let out a slow breath. "Thanks, Bob, and thanks for getting the house ready too." She glanced at the basement door. "You didn't happen to notice any openings in the basement, did you? A broken window or maybe rot around the door?"

"No. Why?"

"When I arrived, a cat was in there. I was wondering whether something needed fixing so other animals don't get in."

Bob frowned and looked at the door. "A cat? Huh. I don't remember seeing any cats. I'll double-check if you want."

"That would be great."

While Bob checked the basement, she called the number he'd given her for Ned and left a message on the answering machine. Hopefully, the leak wouldn't cause a problem with the party plans.

By the time she hung up the phone, Bob had come up from the basement. "I didn't find anything down there."

Julie frowned. "You sure?" If there was no opening, how did the cat get in? The creature hadn't been starving either—not that you could tell by the way it kept demanding food in front of the cabinet—but when she'd picked him up to put him in the carrier, she'd noticed he had some fat on him.

"Yep. But you know cats, they can squeeze into little spaces. I wouldn't worry about it. Come to think of it, it may have run in when I was down there turning the water on, and I didn't notice." He picked up his tool chest. "Well, I better be going. Give me a call if you need anything else."

Bob vacated the kitchen, and the cat trotted in and installed himself in front of the customary cabinet door. That was probably it—the cat had snuck in, and when Bob closed up, it was stuck in the basement. She wondered again whether it belonged to someone, but Myrtle would have called if anyone came in to claim him. Maybe she should double-check again, and also find out if any space had opened up at the animal shelter.

CHAPTER 12

"*What's* this about a party?"

Nolan's heart pinched at the sound of Gramps's words. He didn't want to turn around, as he didn't want to see the grief on Gramps's face, so he forced himself to focus on the coffeepot. "Do you want a coffee?"

"I want you to answer the question."

Nolan did hazard a glance at Gramps's face, then. It was stone.

With an internal sigh, he replaced the coffeepot into its dock and turned with his cup cradled in one hand. Calmly, evenly, he met his grandfather's gaze. "Apparently, they're throwing one last party at the Cozy Holly Inn. Like they used to have on Christmas Eve."

Gramps made a dismissive noise. When he moved

into the kitchen, he showed his age. His gait was stiff, but his shoulders were thrust back, and his chin held high. Nolan pretended not to notice his difficulty. However, Gramps didn't take a chair. He walked up to Nolan instead.

"That Green girl is throwing a party?"

Stan must have told him, unless word was already circulating through town. It might be, given the size of Pinecone Falls and the notoriety of Ida Green's Christmas Eve parties.

"That's what she told me."

Snowball tried to wedge her way in between them without success. When she whined, Nolan dropped his free hand to her head.

Gramps narrowed his eyes. "But why? Ida Green closed down the Cozy Holly Inn."

Nolan nodded. It was a fact, not a question.

"But now her wild granddaughter is here throwing another party."

"I don't know if I'd call her wild—"

Gramps grunted, cutting him off. "I don't like it."

You don't like most things, these days. Nolan wisely kept that thought to himself.

When Gramps looked around the kitchen as if suddenly recalling where he was, he looked weary. He made his way to his customary chair at the kitchen table. His newspaper was there, neatly folded and tucked to one side.

"I think I will take that coffee."

Gramps always had a mug on the go, but he must have been too distracted by the news to bring it with him. Nolan fished a stoneware mug from the cabinet and poured a cup of fragrant, black coffee. He set it in front of his grandfather, who might as well have been a statue.

Nolan almost touched his shoulder—almost. But whatever web of grief and memory Gramps was caught in, he didn't want to interrupt. He didn't want to be drawn into that dark vortex. He had his share of grief over the loss of his mother, too, even if he seemed to be the only member of the family able to come up for breath.

He didn't know what else to say, so he took his coffee cup with him and started toward the work he knew awaited him.

Gramps's voice stopped him in the door.

"Watch her."

Automatically, Nolan looked down at his dog. But it wasn't Snowball that Gramps was talking about. The husky had taken to being Nolan's silent shadow, as she mostly did while they were in Barrington Lodge.

"You mean Julie?" Nolan asked. What in the world was Gramps getting after?

"Yep. You can't trust those Greens. Ida was always up to something, and I bet the granddaughter is no different."

"I'm not going to stalk our neighbor. Do you even hear yourself?"

Gramps scowled. "She's up to something, I tell you. Why go to all that work to clean up the inn and decorate and make food for one party when you aren't even in business?"

At least one inn around here has some Christmas spirit. Nolan didn't say that out loud.

"I take Snowball out in the woods near there every morning." He had no intention of spying on Julie, but maybe this would appease his grandfather. It really was Snowball's favorite path, and he didn't see why he shouldn't continue to do what he'd done every day for years.

"Good," Gramps said.

But from his tone of voice, it sounded as though he meant, *Not good enough.*

CHAPTER 13

The caterer, Jessica, was younger than Julie thought she'd be. She was in her mid-twenties, a robust woman with a ready smile and bright eyes. The moment she stepped into the inn, she said, "Let's see this kitchen."

She sounded, of all things, excited.

Julie led her through the inn, chatting all the while. "Do you cater a lot of events like these?"

"No, not many, but I do a lot of business lunches in the general area. Weddings, anniversaries, sometimes birthdays. I've heard of Ida's Christmas parties, but it's always been my aunt who catered them in the past. And I think Ida did some of the cooking herself."

Julie nodded. "Gram always did love to cook. But

these parties—at least, the way I remember them—they're huge."

Jessica grinned. "You've got half the town, if not more, invited."

Gram was handling the invitations, so Julie had no idea who would come and who wouldn't. Julie grimaced. "I believe it."

"It's so good that you're doing these again. I haven't gone to one, of course—that would be my parents and grandparents—but I've heard stories. It's kind of a tradition in Pinecone Falls."

"It's just this one time. We're—" *selling the property.* Maybe Julie shouldn't air the family's business. She cleared her throat and tried again. "We're not doing them again after that."

Jessica's face fell. "That's too bad. There hasn't been anything in town really to replace it. I was hoping someday to come as a guest, not as the help."

Julie didn't know what to say to that, so she gestured to the kitchen and said, "We're here. Is this a big enough space?"

One thing she would give Jessica, she was not without exuberance when it came to her job. Her face brightened again as she took in the space. "Two commercial ovens! Thank goodness. I was a bit worried. You got the email I sent with the proposed menu? I asked my aunt what Ida used to serve and built it off of that."

Even though the caterer wasn't looking her way, Julie nodded. "I did. But I'm not sure Gram will be able to help out with the cooking this year. We might want to add a little more food, just in case."

"I can email you the options."

Julie nodded. "That would be great. I can call my gram and have her choose something else to flesh out the offerings. We don't want to run out of food!"

Jessica stroked the oven door almost lovingly. "With these, you won't. I'll be able to time the appetizers perfectly so there's always something going around."

Merrow! The cat made his complaint from in front of the door to his food, like usual. Though it sounded a lot like, *What will you bring for me?* to Julie's ears.

Jessica turned with a smile. "Who's this gorgeous fellow?"

When she reached out a hand to pet the cat, Julie tensed. "No, don't…"

The cat shut his eyes and raised his head into the stroke. She could hear his purr even from feet away. He swished his tail and walked forward so Jessica's hand stroked along the arch of his back.

"Don't what?" Jessica asked, still petting him as she pulled her attention away.

Julie shrugged, dumbfounded. "He's a little temperamental, but never mind. He clearly likes you."

More, apparently, than he liked Julie. She felt a little offended but then realized this was good. Maybe it would solve all her problems.

"I don't suppose you're looking for a cat? He needs a good home, and I can't give it to him."

Jessica scratched under the cat's chin. She sighed. "I wish. I love cats, but my apartment doesn't allow pets."

"Tell me about it," Julie muttered.

They shared a moment of silent commiseration.

It was punctuated only by the faint dripping coming from under the sink. Jessica could clearly hear it over the cat's purrs because she frowned. "What's that sound?"

"The kitchen sink. I'm getting it fixed. Don't worry about it."

"I'll need to use the sink while I'm cooking…"

Julie held up her hands. "I promise, it will be fixed before the party."

After a moment's hesitation, Jessica nodded. "Then I guess the only other thing I'll need is to see your temporary event catering permit."

"My… what?"

Julie's stomach sank. Permit? No one had

mentioned that before. She'd just assumed that because Cozy Holly Inn was a bed-and-breakfast that the party would be allowed. But of course, it wasn't actually a working B&B anymore.

Jessica pulled her hand away from the cat. He meowed loudly in protest.

"Your temporary event catering permit."

Julie tried not to panic. "Gram didn't mention that. I can call her…"

She was fishing her phone out of her pocket when Jessica stopped her.

"She might not know. It only became municipal law about five years ago. If you ask me, the town council just wanted a good excuse to collect another fee. But without one, I won't be able to do any cooking on-site."

"And you have to do the cooking on-site?"

"I do. I don't have big enough ovens at home to cook everything, let alone drive it here while it's still hot. But don't worry, it's easy to get one of the permits. All you need to do is call Ted Thorndike and have him come in for an inspection. I can give you his number." She glanced toward the kitchen sink at the *drip, drip, drip* coming from it. "But you might want to get the plumbing fixed first."

The phone in Julie's hand rang. At this point, it was probably more bad news. She glanced at the screen, and it took her a solid two rings to recognize the digits she'd called earlier to reach Ned Wheatley. Relief washed through her, and she held up the phone.

"That won't be a problem. That's the plumber now. If you'll excuse me for just a second?"

Jessica nodded.

Julie couldn't walk far without losing the patch of good cell phone signal, but she moved a few steps away before answering the call. She heard Jessica cooing softly to the cat.

"Hello?"

The pause at the other end of the line was signifi-cant. Julie raised her voice and repeated herself, in case the line was obscured with static on the other end.

"You sound just like your grandmother." The voice on the other end of the line, male, sounded a bit choked up.

"I'm told I look like her too. I'm Julie."

"Yes, Julie, sorry. This is Ned Wheatley. I'm returning your call."

"I'm happy to hear from you. I'm at the inn, and we have a bit of a plumbing problem."

Again, silence on the other end of the line. It didn't comfort her.

"How big of a plumbing problem?"

Julie frowned. "Well, nothing's flooding, but we have a leak under the kitchen sink."

The relief in his voice was palpable. "I can make it out next week to take a look at it."

Julie stared at the phone in her hand for a moment, hoping that she'd heard wrong. She lifted it back to her ear and tried not to screech her answer. "Next *week?*" Panic knotted in her throat, making it difficult to breathe.

"Yes. I'd come out sooner, but there has been more than one emergency in the area, and I'm not as young as I once was. I can only do so much."

Julie grimaced. He sounded, like the handyman, to be around Gram's age—and Gram had been forced to retire because she couldn't keep up with the workload. "I understand that." And she did, even if it didn't help her building panic. "But I have to get an inspector out here for the catering permit, and I don't think we'll pass muster with a leak in the sink."

"Don't you worry about it," Ned assured her. "I know Ted. It won't take him five minutes to do the inspection. If need be, he could even do it the morning of the party, but I don't think it will come to that."

Julie wanted to be reassured, but every muscle in her back was tense. "You've heard about the party."

"Of course! It's wonderful that you're putting it

on one last time. I used to go every year with my brother. But those days are gone now…" He fell silent then cleared his throat. "Tell you what, if you don't mind last-minute notice, I'll come by one day to take a look at the problem. If it's an easy fix, I might be able to do it on the spot."

Julie bit her lip. "And if it isn't?"

"Then we'll at least know how much time it will take. Don't worry, Julie. We'll get you straightened out in time for the party."

Julie wished that she shared his confidence.

CHAPTER 14

The Pinecone Falls café, if it had been situated in the middle of Boston, would have been one of the quaint, mom-and-pop-type establishments swarming with pretentious college students. In Pinecone Falls, the family atmosphere wasn't cultivated to attract hipsters. It was authentic. This small, cozy coffee shop had probably been passed down from parents to children for the last few generations. The art on the walls wasn't from the most up-and-coming artists in Boston hoping to make a name for themselves, but local landscapes, still-lifes, and portraits by local artists who may or may not still be alive. The tables were round, a bit scuffed, and clustered around the main counter where the old-fashioned cash register rested. The air smelled like fresh-baked cookies and cinnamon. It smelled like home.

And, from what Julie could remember from visits in the past, it hadn't changed all that much. But she had, and walking into the small café, she felt like she was trying to fit into clothes from when she'd been a teenager. There was nostalgia, yes. But she felt too large for the space, too different.

"Julie? Julie Green?"

Julie should have been used to people recognizing her in this town by now, but she still startled at the sound of her name. She glanced around until she found the source—a woman her mom's age, with the gray hair and laugh lines to prove it, wearing an apron that wrapped around her hips and carrying a carafe. She smiled warmly.

Julie felt the attention of several other customers in the shop, most of which were her mother's age or older. She forced a smile to her face and pretended not to notice that she was suddenly in the spotlight.

"That's me."

"You look so grown up!"

Julie suddenly found herself wrapped up in a hug from a stranger. She awkwardly hugged back. She'd forgotten that people in small towns didn't have the same sense of personal space boundaries that they did in the city.

. . .

THE STRANGER CLUCKED UNDER HER TONGUE. "You probably don't remember me. I'm Lucy. Back when you were young, I used to waitress here in the summers."

Scattered memories of lunch with Gramps and breakfast with her parents bubbled up. The woman did look familiar. "Yes, I do remember."

Lucy winked. "Now is different. Now I own the place."

"Oh. It's…" Julie glanced around, struggling to find something to say. "It's just as I remember it."

Fortunately, Lucy seemed to take that as a compliment. Still smiling broadly, she asked, "How are Ida and your folks?"

"They're doing well. Gram misses the inn." Julie didn't add that Gram was also sick. No need to put a damper on anyone's day.

Lucy looked sympathetic. "I bet she does. I never thought I'd see the day when Ida Green wasn't up there running the Cozy Holly Inn."

Julie didn't say anything. She didn't know what to say. Instead, she searched the tables in the vain hope that Ivy had reached the café before her.

"Are you meeting someone?"

The question might have been innocent, but it felt

almost sly. Although Julie had been young, she remembered this. The town thrived on gossip. It had to when everyone knew everyone else.

"Ivy."

"Oh." Was it her imagination, or did Lucy sound disappointed? "She's at her usual table in the back. Why don't you sit down, and I'll bring you a menu?"

Julie followed the line of Lucy's arm until she spotted Ivy tucked into a table in the far corner. She raised her hand in a wave when Julie was looking in her direction. Julie thanked Lucy and started toward Ivy. In any café in Boston, this would have taken a matter of seconds.

In Pinecone Falls, Julie was besieged. Some of the people who stopped her on the way she barely recognized. Others were complete strangers. In each case, she stopped and answered the same questions: Yes, her gram was well. No, she wasn't staying in town. She was only here to put together one last party at the inn. Most had heard about the party, of course, and they seemed excited to attend. In a town like Pinecone Falls, any type of get-together was exciting.

By the time she reached the table with Ivy, she felt frazzled. Fortunately, her friend took pity on her and hugged her briefly before they both sat again.

"So, how are things at the inn?"

Julie paused, thinking of how to phrase her latest

problems at the inn. She didn't want to complain or put her problems on Ivy, but she wasn't good at lying and pretending there were no problems either. Apparently, Ivy interpreted the pause accurately.

"That bad, huh?"

Lucy came and handed over exactly one menu. Ivy, it seemed, came here often enough that she didn't need one.

"Thank you." Julie smiled up at Lucy.

"My pleasure. Just flag me down when you're ready to order."

Julie's stomach was already grumbling. Mac and cheese got less appealing by the day, even if it was the only thing she could reliably make without burning. She glanced quickly through the menu as Lucy walked out of earshot again.

Without looking at Ivy, she said, "It's not that bad."

"Right. That's why you can't look me in the eye when you answer the question."

Julie sighed and set down the menu on the table-top. "It's more complicated than I expected it to be, that's all."

"What did you expect?"

"To come, put up some decorations, and that would be that."

"Have you *ever* thrown a party?"

"Not since college." And those were very different than the sort of party Gram wanted.

"How can I help?"

The offer of help was a bit unexpected, and Julie didn't know what to say for a few beats. She glanced around the café. People were, unfortunately, watching her and whispering. But they smiled when she met their eyes. She smiled back and then turned to Ivy.

"I'm sure I can handle it. I just need to get some repairs done to the inn. I have an appointment for that. And, apparently, an inspection. I don't have an appointment for that, yet. And——"

Ivy cut her off as she dug through her purse. "An inspection from Ted Thorndike?"

Julie blinked. "Yes, actually."

"Here. I can give you his number."

"Oh, I think the caterer already did…"

"Did she give you his business line or his cell phone?"

Julie couldn't answer the question. Her friend pounced on that uncertainty.

"Here's his cell phone." She scribbled down a number and slid it across the table. "Tell him you got it from me."

When Julie picked it up, her movements were hesitant. Ivy caught her hand and squeezed. There was nothing in her face but earnest friendliness. For some reason, that surprised Julie. Maybe it shouldn't. She knew Ivy from way back when. But they'd been kids back then. If Julie were to run into any of her old childhood friends in the city, she definitely wouldn't be met with anything other than polite friendliness. Maybe an expressed desire to catch up that never actually came to fruition. Not... this.

Ivy let go of her hand with clear reluctance. "This is a small town. It's not like Boston. Here, people do things to help each other."

And she meant it. If that was really true—and Julie had no reason to think Ivy was lying—then maybe she needed to revise her opinion of Pinecone Falls.

"Actually, there might be something you can do to help?"

Ivy beamed. "What do you need?"

"Do you know where I can find a Christmas tree around here? I remember Gramps just used to chop one down at the edge of the property, but I don't think that's an option this year."

"Why not?"

Julie raised her eyebrows. "I have never chopped down a tree in my life!"

Ivy laughed. "Oh, that's no problem. I'll bring my husband out, and we can do it together."

"You don't have to do that..."

"Don't be silly. I'd love to see what the inn looks like nowadays, anyway."

She and Julie shared a smile.

After they ordered lunch, Ivy asked, "So how is the cat?"

"A menace, as usual."

Ivy smirked as if she didn't believe a word of what Julie was saying.

"He is," she insisted. "He hasn't warmed up to me at all. *And* I had to get him out of a tree the day before yesterday. Well, Nolan did."

Ivy raised her eyebrows suggestively. "Nolan, you say?"

"It was his own fault the cat was up there. His dog chased him up."

"Uh-huh."

Julie glared. "Don't ask me why they were on Gram's property. I mean, I guess their lodge *is* right next door, and with the inn closed—and soon to be his—he's probably used to having the run of the area…"

Ivy leaned her chin on one hand. "And now that you've met him again, what do you think?"

"I think his dog is obnoxious."

Actually, she didn't. When the cat wasn't around, Snowball acted like a perfect gentlewoman. "And he is full of unwanted advice, especially about outerwear."

Ivy laughed loudly, drawing the stares of several people in the café. "He hasn't changed that much, I guess."

Julie couldn't help but smile back. "No, I guess not."

Though he had definitely grown up.

As Lucy arrived with the food and Julie's coffee, Ivy fished through her purse. "Actually, speaking of the cat, I brought a present for him." She pulled out a toy, this one a ball with what looked like a bell on the inside.

Julie couldn't even imagine the amount of noise the cat would make with it. It was sweet of Ivy to bring a gift. "Thank you." She said the same to Lucy, who left them to their conversation.

"Have you thought of a name yet?" Ivy asked.

"You mean 'menace' isn't acceptable?"

Ivy laughed around a bite of her club sandwich. She held her hand in front of her mouth as she chewed and swallowed. "I think you should. Give him a name, I mean. We can't keep calling him The Cat."

"I'm waiting for Myrtle to call with an opening at the shelter," Julie reminded her.

"If he's such a menace, you're not in danger of getting attached." Ivy took another bite, chewed, and swallowed before she said, "Why not call him Kringle?"

"Kringle?"

"For the holiday season."

Julie thought for a second about how the white cat would look, tangled up in Christmas lights. She couldn't help but smile. "Okay, fine. You win. We'll call him Kringle. *For now.*"

Her mouth was full when another woman, close to ninety if her stooped posture and shuffling gait were any indication, shouted loud enough to wake the dead.

"Lucy, I still have hands. I still have feet. I can serve my customers. Or are you trying to make me older than I already am?"

Julie bit her lip to keep from snickering. It was exactly the sort of thing Gram would say.

The old woman—and if Julie squinted, she could almost make out a familiarity in the woman's face from her visits to Pinecone Falls during the summers—took the carafe from Lucy's hands and turned away. She wore thick glasses and a smug, if friendly, smile as she turned toward those seated at the nearest table, only two away from where Ivy and Julie were seated. She topped off both their cups without asking whether they wanted a refill.

Julie leaned forward and whispered to Ivy, "I thought Lucy was the owner now."

"Yes, but she had to wrestle the business out of her mother's hands. Maura did not want to retire."

Julie raised one shoulder in a shrug. "Neither did Gram."

Despite the slow movements that came with age, Maura reached their table with surprising quickness. As she refilled both Ivy's and Julie's cups in turn, she hummed under her breath.

When she looked at Julie's face, the humming stopped abruptly.

"Ida?"

Julie winced. "Not quite. Ida is my gram."

"Of course!" Her face had brightened, and it made her look younger. "You're back at the inn!"

"For a little while," Julie hedged.

"Oh, it will be so nice to see the place up and running again. The town hasn't been the same without it."

"I'm not running the inn." Julie held up her hands to stave off that idea. Who was spreading *that* rumor? "I'm just helping to throw the Christmas party, and then I'm going back to Boston. Gram won't be staying either."

Maura leaned closer, her face almost conspiratorial. "Are you getting one of those newfangled websites? Can't understand those things myself, but it seems if you're going to attract business from out of town, you have to have one these days."

"I don't…"

Maura pinched Julie's cheek affectionately. She felt about twelve. "It's good you're here again. I'm sure you'll be able to do your gram proud."

Whatever Julie planned to say to that was lost in the watery warmth sloshing around inside her chest. Somehow, she managed to choke out a thank-you. Maura went on her way, her humming cheerful and off-key.

Julie pinched the bridge of her nose. Who *had* told Maura that Julie was staying in town to run the inn? Then again, the old woman had clearly seemed confused. At first, she'd seemed to think Julie *was* Gram, though she hadn't by the end.

"What's this about you staying in town?"

The voice froze Julie's warm thoughts. Nolan Miller was looming over the table. She hadn't noticed him come into the café, but his presence wasn't something that anyone could overlook now. The silence and craned necks from the other tables attested that much.

Sitting, Julie felt at a disadvantage, but she wasn't going to let him intimidate her. She crossed her arms. "I told you, I'm not."

CHRISTMAS AT COZY HOLLY INN

"I know what you told me, but apparently, that's not what Maura seemed to think. What kind of game are you playing? Is this some kind of trick to force Gramps to pay more for the property? Because it *isn't* going to work."

Julie gritted her teeth. The nerve! And just when she was starting to think that he wasn't so bad. "It isn't a trick. Or a game. I told you, I'm here for the party. Nothing else."

He crossed his arms, mimicking her pose, though with a good deal more attitude thrown in. "I don't believe you."

"Believe whatever you want," she snapped. "It won't change the facts."

And with that dour cloud over her lovely afternoon, she turned to Ivy.

"Thank you for lunch. I think I'd better get back to the inn."

Ivy didn't stand to hug her this time, which was just as well, because Julie wasn't in the mood. She stormed out of the café and started toward her rented truck. She paused as she noticed the shoe store two shops down.

Out of spite, she went in and bought a pair of winter boots more appropriate to the snowdrifts of Vermont. The reminiscences of the shop owner about the parties thrown at the Cozy Holly Inn were, this time, a balm to Julie's wounded pride.

She was here for one reason only: to throw one last Christmas Eve party. And she was going to make it the best party the Cozy Holly Inn had ever seen, but she couldn't do that with frozen feet.

CHAPTER 15

*J*ulie hummed Christmas songs under the disapproving eye of her feline shadow as she put the finishing touches on the decorations on the first floor. She felt accomplished in a way she usually only felt when delivering a particularly challenging article. The second floor and bathrooms were now as spotless as the first floor, and all of the indoor decorations had been laid out, save for the ones reserved for the tree. She had boughs of artificial holly, brightly colored garlands, indoor lights strung around the windowsills, and snowflake decals in the windows. But that hadn't been enough, to her eye.

With an unrestrained smile, she straightened the fresh pine boughs she had cut from a tree outside. Arranged artfully on the mantel with a red candle in the center as decoration, they looked cheery and welcoming. The scent of fresh pine mixed with the subtle smell of cinnamon from the candle in a way that said, to Julie, *Christmas*.

The cat started to hack up a hairball.

Turning, she braced her hands on her hips and glared at him. "I don't need your approval. This party isn't for you. You won't even be here."

The hairball spilled onto the wood floor, diminishing Julie's holiday cheer. Grimacing, she retreated to the kitchen for paper towels to clean it up.

When she returned to the kitchen with the mess to toss it in the garbage, the cat was sitting in front of the cabinet that held his food. He mewled hopefully.

"Oh, no," she said, shaking her head. "Judging by what happened in the other room, your stomach is suspect right now."

The look he gave her would have stopped traffic. She wilted. "It's not time yet."

If anything, his eyes seemed to grow even bigger and more baleful.

"Fine." She opened the cabinet door and scooped half a can into his dish.

She watched the cat make a show of sniffing suspiciously at the food as she consulted her to-do list. The next item was to call Ted Thorndike about the inspection. She had been too wound up to do it first thing when she'd gotten back, even though it was the item that would take the smaller amount of time. First, she'd needed to work off her frustration over the way Nolan Miller had acted. Did he really think she was up to something? It was strange, almost as if someone had put the idea in his head, because his attitude prior had been neighborly. Oh well, she really didn't care what he thought.

Before she could dial Ted's number, her phone rang. It was Cheryl, and she felt a momentary pang of guilt for not updating her on her progress.

"You haven't texted!"

"I know, I'm sorry! I've been so busy with the party."

"I know, you've probably slowed down to a small-town-life pace."

"Very funny. This party is a bit more work than I envisioned. I've had repair guys and caterers and inspectors and plumbers to call and see. Not to mention putting this place in order. You have no idea how much dust a place can accumulate in only a couple years."

"I'll bet." Cheryl laughed.

"Plus, I've had to run into town a couple times. And that always involves talking to literally everyone I see. I guess I look a lot like my grandmother because they all seem to recognize me. Some even remember me from when I was a kid."

Cheryl groaned. "Oh, that's the worst! I do not envy you. I'd rather be in the city any day, where I can go about my business without everyone in town wanting to know what that business is."

"It wasn't that bad."

"Uh-huh." Cheryl did not sound as though she believed her.

The thing was, Julie was surprisingly enough telling the truth. Aside from her run-in with Nolan, everyone had been friendly. It was nice to be met with smiles instead of people pretending she didn't exist— or worse, that she was a nuisance and in the way. But maybe she didn't need to mention that to Cheryl.

Instead, she said, "No, really. I went out to lunch with an old friend from back when I used to visit here. She owns the pet store now. It was really nice to catch up."

"Well, that's different," Cheryl insisted. "Friends are friends. If a stranger came up to talk to you, that's way different. Anyway, I actually called because I have some good news." Cheryl's voice took on a singsong quality.

"Oh?"

"HR has started making callbacks for interviews."

Julie's stomach cramped. "I haven't gotten a call." At least, not that she knew of. Maybe she should double-check her voicemail, just in case.

"No, you wouldn't have."

"Then how is this good news?"

"It's good news because I happened to stop in and take a peek at the résumés still in the running."

"Couldn't that cost you your job?"

"What? Of course not. I didn't go through them, I just took a look to see what was on top. And guess what? It's yours."

Julie's stomach tightened again. This time, with something closer to anticipation than nerves. "So I'm next to get the call?"

"That would be my guess. She's already cleaned off her desk of applicants they're definitely not considering."

"That's… that's really good news."

Wasn't it? Julie didn't feel as excited as she thought she would. That was probably because she was so mired in trying to make this party a success that she didn't have time to be anxious about what she would say on a phone call to HR. Those were, essentially, preliminary interviews. Julie was not prepared for this.

"You should be saying, 'Thank you, Cheryl.'"

Julie smiled and repeated the words. "Thank you, Cheryl. I mean it. But now I'm nervous. And I have to go—more phone calls to make about this party."

"Ugh. I can't *wait* for it to be over and for you to come back home. Text me."

"I will," Julie promised.

The silence in the kitchen after she hung up the phone was oppressive. Shouldn't she be more excited about the possibility of an interview? This was the job she wanted. But right now, it just felt like one more responsibility.

She opened her to-do list and added one more item: *prepare for possible interview.*

Then she set about checking off the item just above it. She used the number Ivy had given her to reach Ted. He answered on the third ring.

"Hello?"

"Ted Thorndike?"

"That's me."

Nervous insects took wing in her stomach. This shouldn't be hard. All she needed was a last-minute inspection. She cleared her throat as softly as she could. In the background, she could hear the cat lapping up the cat food and purring.

"I'm Julie Green, Ida's granddaughter."

"Oh, Ida! How is the old bird?"

Ted's friendly tone and the familiarity relaxed her.

Even if she did have to fudge the truth a bit by omitting the fact that Gram was sick.

It's just a little cough. But it could be more than that. Pneumonia, or worse…

Don't think about it. If it was serious, Gram would go to the hospital.

Julie only half believed herself.

"She's good," she said, hoping her voice didn't sound as thin on the other end as it did to her ears. "She misses the inn, though. Actually, I'm here in town to help her put on one last Christmas Eve party."

"I heard, and I imagine you'll be needing a permit, then."

Relief sagged her shoulders. "Yes. A temporary catering permit."

"I can run out there tomorrow."

That would have been a relief *if* she'd had the plumbing fixed. "Actually, tomorrow isn't good. You see, there's a problem with the plumbing I need to get fixed, and there's a chance Ned won't make it out until the twenty-third. I don't suppose there's any chance you could do the inspection the morning of the party?"

She held her breath.

Fortunately, Ted's response was instant and confident. "No problem. I have nothing booked on

Christmas Eve. As long as you get that plumbing issue seen to beforehand, it'll be smooth sailing."

"Thank you so much. I really appreciate it."

Ted chuckled. "It's no problem, honestly. I'll get the paperwork started so all I have to do is sign off on the permit the day of. I'm pretty sure the town would string me up if I was the reason you couldn't put on one of Ida's parties."

Julie wasn't great at small talk, but she managed a few friendly words with Ted, mostly about how her Gram was finding retirement, before she disconnected the call. Her relief was palpable. This was all going to work out.

She crossed *Talk to Ted about the permit* off of her to-do list.

CHAPTER 16

*N*olan was not usually a suspicious person. He felt bad about his conversation with Julie. Maybe his father's and grandfather's grumpy distrustful attitudes were rubbing off. He hoped not. On the other hand, he did see some holes in Julie's story that she wasn't staying in town. Here she was meeting with friends and talking to people in the diner as if she were planning to be part of the community. And she was having a party at the inn. That sounded like something to do for a grand opening. And she had a cat!

But the biggest thing was that he'd heard a rumor while he was at the feed store that the inn was opening back up, Ida was coming back, and Julie was staying to help her.

And would it be so bad if she did stay in town?

There was something about her, even as prickly as she was, that made Nolan want to like her. Someone who liked animals as much as she did—and he did remember the cat she'd brought with her everywhere as a kid—couldn't be bad.

She'd grown up into a very attractive woman. Nolan didn't usually feel this tug toward women, maybe because he knew everyone in town and would have had to drive a good distance in order to meet someone new. He didn't bother, since he hadn't really wanted to date after his last disastrous relationship and his mom's death. But Julie…

If what she said was true, she would be out of Pinecone Falls soon enough.

Nolan cleared his throat. Family dinners were always awkward these days, with conversation scratching the surface of superficial. The weather, the guests, problems with the inn. All spaced between long silences. The lodge didn't offer dinner to the guests, just breakfast, so Nolan usually did the cooking for the three of them. It didn't help that Nolan wasn't the cook his mother had been, and half the time he managed to burn dinner while trying to do three other things.

Tonight's roast beef wasn't half bad, mostly because he'd remembered to set a timer on his phone, and he'd opened a can of beef gravy to go alongside it and the potatoes instead of trying—and failing—to make it from the beef drippings. Still, he found he didn't have an appetite. He set his fork down on his plate with an audible *clink*.

Stan narrowed his eyes. "Something got into you?"

Nolan sighed. He knew better than to read too much into town gossip, but this could be important to his family. "I heard a rumor while I was in town today about Julie Green."

Silence.

Gramps set down his knife and fork with a lot more grace than Nolan had. "What about her?"

"I heard she might be staying on longer than the party."

Gramps narrowed his eyes. His face might as well have been carved from stone. "How long?"

"I don't know. It was only a rumor. It wasn't specific." He didn't want to add in the part about Ida coming back and rile Gramps up further. Trying to get back to what should have been a normal dinner, he speared a wedge of potato. He didn't lift it to his mouth. "Gramps, are you *sure* this sale is going through?"

Gramps wanted this sale so badly, and Nolan didn't want to see him disappointed. But the evidence was pointing to some ugliness in the near future with the Greens. If Ida Green had been in any way capable of running the inn herself, or if her son and daughter-in-law had been willing to take up the responsibility rather than jetting around the world, the property wouldn't have been put up for sale in the first place. But Julie Green had never before been a concern. She'd been distant, so distant she hadn't even visited except briefly at Christmas. Nolan would have thought she had no interest in the property either.

But now that he'd met her, he had to wonder…

"Yes," Gramps said with a grunt. "I'm sure. Ida and I have had our differences, but I have her this time."

Nolan decided he didn't want to know what those differences had been. Gramps had always had a chip on his shoulder when it had come to the Cozy Holly Inn. Nolan had always assumed it was because Ida Green was an old business rival, but maybe that wasn't the case…

He hesitated just long enough for the two older men to mark it. With an inner sigh, he figured he might as well put all his worries out on the table.

"I saw her in town today. Julie. She was talking to Ivy—the pet store owner—about some sort of permit. I didn't catch the whole conversation, but when someone came up to her and talked about her

CHRISTMAS AT COZY HOLLY INN

staying, I figured it couldn't hurt to straighten out the facts. I asked her point-blank whether she was planning on staying past the party."

His dad had stopped eating now too. "And?"

Nolan shrugged. "And she said no."

"But you don't believe her."

"Those Greens," Gramps muttered under his breath darkly.

Nolan pretended not to hear. "Why would she need a permit unless she was planning on opening up to customers again?"

Gramps harrumphed. "Good question. Well, I know one person I can ask. I owe Ted Thorndike a favor. Maybe it's time to repay him. I may be able to learn more about what the Greens are up to at the same time."

Nolan was confused. "So, the sale isn't final, then?"

Silence.

Reluctantly, Stan admitted, "No. There was a P&S signed, but Ida can still back out, though she'd forfeit her deposit."

"That old bird is up to something," Gramps muttered. "I don't like it."

Nolan did *not* want to get in the middle of this. Maybe he should have kept his mouth shut.

Gramps turned to him with a calculating look. "I

think we need to watch this Julie character a little closer. Maybe it's time you took a walk after dinner."

Nolan glanced at Snowball whose ears had perked up at the word "walk." They usually did walk after dinner, though he'd been steering clear of the Cozy Holly Inn property since the last incident. "I am going for a walk, but I'm not going to peek in windows or try to listen to conversations, and I'm sticking to our side of the property line."

Gramps snorted. "Maybe you could step over the line a little bit, and if you happened to see or hear something... well... that might tell us something about their intentions. That's all I was expecting."

❄

"YOU SOUND BETTER," JULIE SAID INTO THE PHONE. It was a relief to hear Gram without a fit of coughing interrupting her. She shifted on the rickety chair at the kitchen table, keeping one eye on the pot of water she was waiting to boil for her night's mac and cheese.

"I told you it was nothing to worry about," Gram said firmly.

"I'm glad." Julie didn't tell her grandmother that she had been and still was worried. Gram would just brush it off as usual.

"I've sent out the invitations."

At least that was one thing Julie wouldn't have to worry about. She crossed her legs. The cat, lying on his back on the kitchen floor, batted playfully at the new toy Ivy had given him.

"Oh? Who's coming?"

"Not as many people as usual," Gram answered. "And *not* the Millers. I don't want that grouch of a man to ruin the party."

"Which man would that be?" Julie asked. Gram couldn't possibly mean Nolan. Gram hadn't seen him in years, and even though he'd been frosty in town today, he usually made an effort at being civil. She couldn't picture him being grouchy to Gram. He seemed like the type of guy that would be kind to grandmothers.

"Klaus. He's only gotten worse with the years."

"That would be Nolan's grandfather?"

Gram hesitated before answering. "You've met Nolan?"

"I knew Nolan from my trips here as a kid."

Julie didn't know why she was avoiding the question. Maybe because when she thought of Nolan, she didn't think of the cold way he'd treated her in town today. She thought of the breadth of his shoulders and the indulgent smile he gave his dog. Or maybe it was the hopeful tone in her grandmother's voice.

Julie cleared her throat and added, more softly, "But yes, I ran into him again. He walks his dog along the property."

"His or ours?"

"Both."

"Has he given you any trouble?"

"No," she lied. "In fact, he saved the cat from a tree the other day."

She didn't mention that his dog had been responsible for the cat's climb in the first place.

"Well, Nolan always seemed to take after his mother more so than the men in his family. He's a good boy."

Julie chuckled. "He's a man now, Gram. Not a little boy."

"So, you've noticed?"

Oh, no. Julie didn't want to get this from Gram as well as Ivy. She said, "Weren't we talking about the party? You didn't say who you invited."

"Oh, I don't think you'd recognize the names, dear. A lot of old friends, but not nearly as many people as I'd usually invite. We don't have the rooms available to rent. Though it might be a good idea for you to ready a few of them just in case someone drinks too much of Great-Grandma's famous rum punch and can't drive home."

"I'll make sure to get several ready." It sounded

like most of the people coming to the party would be from Gram's generation. Not that Julie minded. This *was* a party specifically for Gram, after all. But maybe she could sneak in one more invite. "Can I invite Ivy and her husband? They've volunteered to help cut down a tree to bring inside."

"Oh, that's nice. I'm so glad that you've been able to reconnect with an old friend. You and Ivy used to be inseparable."

"I'm glad too. It's really nice to see her again." It brought back all the fuzzy memories of when she'd used to spend the summers in Pinecone Falls. The Cozy Holly Inn had been Julie's favorite place in the world until she'd become a teenager, and her social life hadn't left much room for month-long visits.

"The best trees are out back near the stream, at the edge of the property. But be careful. That's close to Klaus's property, and he might give you some trouble. He's always been a sore loser. His son too. Maybe even his grandson. Be careful."

That word of advice was directly opposed to what she'd said of Nolan only minutes before, but Julie held her tongue. Mostly because she agreed. The apple couldn't possibly have fallen that far from the tree.

But with Ivy and her husband with her, Julie hoped she wouldn't have any trouble.

CHAPTER 17

inally, a day that actually went according to plan. Not only had Julie made a large dent in cleaning the rooms upstairs and putting fresh linens on the beds, but she'd gotten a last-minute call from Ned Wheatley. He could stop by.

He was older than even Gram, if Julie had to guess. It was hard not to hover over him as he lowered himself to the floor of the kitchen and tried to wedge his way beneath the sink to look at the pipes. Now she understood why he hadn't been certain he could fit her in. Judging by the way his joints creaked and popped, she doubted he could try to fit himself under too many cabinets in one day.

But, despite his frailness, he was a friendly man. The gray hair thinning on top of his head showed age spots underneath. He was still relatively trim, and he moved unaided by cane or walker, as many his age would have needed. His shoulders were bowed, but he held himself with pride, nevertheless.

As he splayed himself fully onto the floor, the cat came up to paw ineffectually at the cabinet holding his food. Julie tossed one of his toys down the hall. "Go away. Go play. I don't need you getting in Ned's way."

Ned chuckled. "Oh, don't worry about me. He seems like a sweet little dog." He held out his hand to the cat to sniff. The cat turned tail and retreated out of the kitchen. His posture practically bled disdain.

Dog? Hopefully, Ned's eyesight wasn't so bad that he couldn't fix the leak. Maybe he could only see tufts of fur from his vantage point and not the whole animal.

Julie sat at the kitchen table and tried not to fidget. "Do you need some help?"

"No, no," Ned said, though he was still trying to wedge his way underneath the sink to see properly with the flashlight he held in one hand.

Julie jiggled her foot then forced herself to stop.

"It's been such a long time since I've been here," Ned said, his voice wistful. "My brother and I used to come to the Christmas Eve party every year. He's gone now. I'll be happy to go one last time for us both, but it won't be the same."

"I'm sorry," Julie said softly.

"Thank you. It wasn't that long ago that we lost him. Pneumonia, last winter. Terrible thing."

Julie thought of Gram's cough and swallowed heavily.

"But when we were younger, we used to get fully into the Christmas spirit. Neil and I used to dress up as elves and help Ida hand out the little gifts she liked to prepare."

Gifts? She made a note on her phone to ask Gram about these gifts.

"We're twins, you see. No one could tell us apart in our younger days." Ned sighed. "Those were the days…"

"It sounds like they were fun." Julie felt a pang of sympathy. She couldn't ease the pain of his loss, and strangely enough, she wanted to.

She wondered whether she could find one of those little elf decorations at one of the local stores, to put into Ned's gift. Gram would have invited him for sure.

"Ah. I see your problem here."

"You do?" Julie hadn't noticed when Ned had managed to fit himself under the sink, but she could only see him from the chest down. He'd set down the flashlight in the corner of the open cabinet door and was using both his hands and some of the tools he'd brought with him while he fiddled beneath the sink.

"Yes. This bolt here looks like it's rusted through, and the threading might have gone on the pipe too. I might need to replace the whole thing. The electrical wiring here is old. You should have it moved."

Electrical wiring obviously didn't fall under the purview of plumbing. And come to think of it, why was it run beneath the sink to begin with? The house had been built before formal inspections when people took shortcuts.

"Will the electrical affect the inspection? I still need to get the temporary catering permit."

Ned grunted then slowly pulled himself out from beneath the sink. He replaced the bucket she'd put beneath the tap but didn't turn the water back on. Flat on his back on the floor, he answered, "No. Just something that needs doing, and sooner rather than later, I'd say."

Then, in Julie's opinion, it was something for Klaus Miller to worry about. He was willing to buy the property as is, after all. He could fix it up.

Unless… what if he'd already decided to have the house torn down instead?

The thought hit Julie like a punch. Julie breathed shallowly through her mouth. She didn't like the twist of emotion that wrenched through her chest at the thought. This inn was her childhood. It was her family's legacy.

At least, it had been. But Gram couldn't keep it up anymore. The Cozy Holly Inn was closed. It would never open to customers again, at least not under her family's ownership.

Except for one last Christmas Eve party.

Still, Julie had just sort of assumed that Klaus would make the repairs and bring it back to functioning as an inn.

Julie squared her shoulders. "What about the plumbing? Can you fix that?"

"Yes, but not today."

Julie tried not to show her dismay, but she must have failed.

He added, "I don't have the parts. I'll have to pick them up, and I'll give you a call when I have the time to come back. We'll get it done before the party, don't you worry."

With a groan she pretended not to notice for the sake of his dignity, he pulled himself into a sitting position and reached out to pat her hand. His skin was surprisingly smooth, considering his line of work. She smiled at him.

"Do you need some help up?"

"No, no. I can do it myself."

Privately, Julie had other opinions, but she didn't

offer again. She did help by returning his tools, including the flashlight, to his toolkit. She offered the heavy case to him when he was standing.

Then she let him precede her down the hall to the front door, where he'd left his coat on the brass coatrack in the foyer. His heavy boots made imprints on the floor, but there was no way she'd been willing to tell him to take them off when he'd arrived. They were the kind that tied up to the ankles and probably took twenty minutes to tie or untie.

"Tell me more about these gifts Gram used to give out during the party?"

"Oh, maybe gifts was the wrong word. Party favors? They were small little things really, but they made the evening an extra something special."

His answer made her feel only marginally more prepared. For Christmas party favors, she might put together anything from tree ornaments to Christmas cookies and candy canes. Actually, given her skill with baking—or the utter lack thereof—ornaments were looking very appealing. If she could find a ninety-nine-cent store that carried clear glass ornaments, she could cut up strips of wrapping paper and arrange them inside like swirls of ribbon. Maybe add the year of the party on the front with a paint pen or the words *Cozy Holly Inn*. It would be something for Gram to remember the season too. Humming under her breath, Julie lagged behind to add the idea to her to-do list and grab a picture off the internet that illustrated the idea.

The internet, of course, was glacial out here near the living room.

"What a good boy you are," Ned cooed ahead of her. He must have found the cat.

Julie held her phone in the air, even though she knew it probably wouldn't help to find a better data signal.

Ned continued, "Waiting all this time for me to finish and not a bark from you. Here you go, you can go do your business."

"What?" Julie shoved the phone into the pocket of her jeans. She glanced up in horror as Ned was opening the front door. "No, don't—"

Too late. The cat bolted for freedom. Julie bit her cheek to keep from swearing. A white cat romping in the snow? It would probably take her a good half an hour to find him again—and that, only *if* he wanted to be found.

She could leave him out there.

Bobcats. Bobcats, and freezing to death.

The loud bark of a dog froze her blood. "Oh, no. Not again."

Without thinking, she brushed past Ned and slammed her sock feet into her new boots. As she reached the porch, one of the boots crumpled uncomfortably beneath her heel, she stopped to call after the cat.

"Cat! Cat!" Right. Hadn't Ivy given him a name? "Kringle!"

Even though Julie hadn't even called the cat by name yet, that word made him pause. Or maybe it was the dog in his path that had caused that.

Kringle stood in the path of her footsteps from an earlier excursion outside, his back arched. Opposite Kringle, Snowball had her rump in the air and her tail sweeping the drifts. Snowball gave a playful bark.

Apparently, Kringle wasn't in a playful mood. He reared back and swatted the dog across the nose.

Yipe!

Julie winced as a red streak marred the white fur on Snowball's nose. The dog whimpered and retreated a step.

Desperate, Julie shouted, "Kringle!"

The cat glanced at her with a wide-eyed look. To her surprise, he trotted to the porch. She met him at the bottom of the stairs and tried to lift him into her arms, only to earn herself a scratch and a hiss for her efforts. He fled up the stairs behind her.

Nolan, likewise, called for his dog. When Julie straightened, their eyes met. She didn't know what her expression looked like. His gaze flicked to Snowball, who was slinking through the snow toward him, head lowered.

Julie trotted over to the edge of the nearest snowbank. "I'm sorry if Kringle hurt her."

And she was. Snowball seemed like a nice dog, if overly enthusiastic when it came to cats. The curl of her tail beneath her rump made Julie feel like she'd slapped the dog herself.

"It's fine." The dog reached Nolan, who patted her gently on the head and crouched in front of her to look at her nose.

"Do you want to come inside? I have a first aid kit."

"No." He straightened and patted his thigh. "Come on, Snowball." Before he turned away, he looked up at Julie and added, "Don't worry about it. It was our fault. Snowball ran over when she saw Kringle. Guess she needs to learn that not all creatures love to play."

Nolan left, and Julie hurried up the porch to where the cat was huddled next to the closed door. Ned was on the porch, trying to lean down to pat the cat, who looked distinctly like he was going to bite the old man's hand.

"I'm sorry, Ned. I think he might be hurt. I don't mean to rush you out…"

"It's fine." Ned straightened, though he looked

concerned. "If he's hurt, maybe you should take him down to the vet."

"I don't have an appointment—I've never even taken him to the vet there before."

Ned shook his head. "It doesn't matter. Susan will make room in her schedule for emergencies. We take care of each other here."

Julie met his gaze then smiled. She thought Kringle was more shaken than anything else, but it felt good to know that there was a safety net in town if ever she needed one. Keeping one eye on the cat, she opened the door to the house wide enough for him to slink inside.

As he did, she noticed his limp and revised her opinion about going to the vet. How would he find a new family if he had an injury? Besides, Kringle might not be her cat, but there was no way she was going to leave him injured and in pain.

Even if he did give her three new scratches as she reintroduced him to the cat carrier.

CHAPTER 18

olan jiggled his knee as he waited in one of the uncomfortable plastic chairs of the Pinecone Falls Veterinary Services waiting room. He'd long since learned that if he was in the room with Snowball while she was being examined, she would only whimper more to catch his attention. She behaved better for Susan if he was outside of the room. And, given how deep those scratches along her snout looked, he needed her to be on her best behavior.

He was the only person in the waiting room. The receptionist had run out to grab lunch, and the vet technician was in with Susan, helping to hold Snowball still while her nose was cleaned and examined. Nolan had already flipped through the magazines next to the chairs, all pet-themed, and was growing more nervous by the minute. Hadn't they been in there long enough? What if there was a problem? That scratch had caught the corner of Snowball's nose itself, and he knew dogs' noses were very sensitive.

Of course, it was his own fault. He'd noticed a second truck parked at the Cozy Holly Inn and had ventured over the property line to investigate. The cat had run out, and Snowball seized the opportunity for a new playmate.

He took a breath, smelling the fresh pine boughs that were arranged along the top of the counter. The smell of Christmas. He missed that smell at the lodge.

A huge tree strung with lights, candy canes, and plastic ornaments of animals was stuffed into one corner. Paper snowflakes hung at intervals from the ceiling—with his height, he'd already walked into one. The walls were papered with printouts of cats and dogs in winter gear or Santa hats, colored and signed by the local elementary school children. It was cheery and welcoming and exactly the way he wanted Barrington Lodge to feel. That was how it used to be on Christmas when his mother was alive. But how could he persuade his dad and grandfather to get back into the spirit? Nolan hadn't had much success on that front so far.

The door opened, and Nolan, slouched in the

chair, turned to look at who had entered. He stiffened when Julie stopped on the threshold, cat carrier in hand.

"Oh." Julie's gaze flicked from Nolan's face to the floor, searching for Snowball. "Is Snowball okay?"

"Just a few scratches. I'm sure she'll be fine." Her sincere look and obvious concern at the prospect that the dog was not okay overshadowed Nolan's previous suspicions that she was up to something. Those suspicions had come from his grandfather and a small-town rumor. Maybe he should consider the source. His gut instinct was telling him that Julie really was concerned.

Meow!

Nolan narrowed his gaze on the carrier. "Is the cat okay?" The cat had seemed fine when he fled to the porch of the inn, but Nolan would feel terrible if Snowball had done any damage.

"Kringle is his name." Julie sat a few chairs away, placed the carrier on the floor, then bent to look inside. "He was limping a little, so I thought I should bring him."

"I hope he's okay."

"Me too."

They lapsed into an awkward silence. Suddenly very warm, Nolan unzipped his jacket.

Julie glanced over, breaking the silence when she

recognized the logo on his T-shirt. "You went to Northeastern University? Which campus?"

The question broke the tension between them. It turned out that not only had they attended the same school, albeit for different degrees—his in American history, hers in journalism—but they'd graduated only a year apart. As they compared notes on the teachers they'd liked and loathed, Julie switched to a seat closer to him. She warmed to the conversation, her eyes sparkling, and her cheeks flushed as she leaned closer to him. He might have been flushing a little, himself. She was very pretty.

And, surprisingly, she also had an interest in American history, even if she hadn't chosen to get her degree in it. They had definitely taken some of the same courses, though maybe not in the same semester. It had been so long since he'd thought about his college days, and he couldn't help but be disappointed. There she'd been, so close, and yet they'd never crossed paths.

When the conversation naturally petered out, he decided to get the truth out of her while they were meeting on neutral ground. Not only for his family's sake—right now, he wanted to know too. "The Cozy Holly Inn will probably need a lot of work if you intend to stay on instead of selling it."

She sighed and crossed her arms. "Tell me about it. But I'm *not* staying on."

"No?"

"No," she said firmly. "Let's just say small-town life is not for me. I've got a résumé out for a job that would be a great next step for my career. See?"

Although he hadn't asked, she pulled out her phone and opened an email. It was a confirmation of receipt of a résumé for a magazine name he vaguely recognized.

"Oh, that's great. I heard a rumor your grand-mother was coming back to run the inn with your help. Crazy small-town rumors."

"Yeah, very crazy. Funny you say that, because I get the impression people around town think I'm staying too. But don't worry, I'm not. We're selling the inn to you guys just as planned."

"Right." Instead of feeling glad about that, Nolan felt disappointed.

Their eyes caught and held. Nolan felt the smile slide off his face. He wanted to say something, but he wasn't sure what. The examination room door opened, saving him from thinking about it any further.

"Here we are, Nolan. All better."

Snowball did not look better. She looked miserable.

Her head was lowered, framed by a plastic cone that would presumably keep her from rubbing away the bandage across her snout. Her tail was tucked between her legs, and her ears were pinned to her head.

"Oh, no. Snowball!" Julie moved first, closing the distance to the dog and crouching next to her head. "You poor thing. I knew that scratch looked bad."

Susan, the town vet, raised her eyebrows at Nolan. She held Snowball's leash loosely in her hand. The dog didn't seem likely to bolt, but she did give her tail a half-hearted wag when Julie gently petted her ears.

If Julie could get through her misery at all, Snowball must like her. And anyone Snowball liked couldn't be all bad.

Susan cleared her throat and said, "It wasn't a deep cut, but I bandaged it to keep it from getting infected. I know you, Nolan. Leave the cone on at least until this evening."

He gave her a rueful smile but didn't make any promises. Instead, he stood and zipped up his coat before holding his hand out for the leash. "You'll send the bill to the house?"

Susan nodded.

"Thanks." He met Julie's gaze once more. He didn't know what she felt, but he was kicking himself for having misjudged her when they'd met again. He gave her a nod. "Let me know how Kringle makes out."

If Kringle was injured, it would be his fault. He'd pay the bill, but he had the feeling that Julie was the type that didn't like other people paying for her. He didn't want to argue about it. Better to call the clinic from his truck and let Tina, the receptionist, know. Maybe he'd even instruct her to pretend it was paid for by a fund the animal shelter had in place with the veterinarian.

As he reached the door, Susan called after him. "Nolan?"

He stopped.

"I saw you stop by at our volunteer vaccination clinic last month."

Heat crept up his neck, but he tried not to show his embarrassment. Instead, he shrugged. "I do have a dog."

"And you and I both know she didn't need a free rabies vaccine. Thank you for your donation to the Pets in Need Fund. Are you sure you don't want your name on the wall of donors?"

"I'm sure. I wasn't here on behalf of Barrington Lodge." He didn't know why people felt the need to shout when they gave what they could spare to a good cause, but Nolan preferred to give where he could, how he could, without all the spotlight falling on him.

"If you're sure…"

"Yeah. Thanks, Susan," he said, raising the leash to indicate Snowball. When he opened the door, the dog begrudgingly followed him out of the vet, looking morose all the while.

Before the door swung shut, he heard Susan ask, "And who do we have here?"

"The monster who put the scratch on Snowball's nose."

Nolan smiled to himself and unlocked his truck.

❄

JULIE STARED AFTER NOLAN'S RETREATING BACK, something in her softening. Okay, yes, he'd been annoying with his comment about her not remembering what winter was like when they'd first met, and he had acted a bit jerk-like in the diner. But, truth be told, the new boots were keeping her feet much warmer than her ruined suede ones, and now that he'd mentioned the rumor about her staying, she guessed she could kind of see why he had been angry. She might have been, too, if the roles were reversed and her gram thought she had a deal with the Millers, only to find out they were planning to renege on it behind her back.

Plus, he'd seemed so embarrassed to be put in the

spotlight for the donation he'd made. It was cute. A lot of people would have used that donation as a stepping-stone to make them seem like they were better people.

Maybe Nolan was a genuinely good person, so much so that he didn't have to prove it to himself or to other people.

"Oh, I'm sure that's not true."

"Hmm?"

The vet, Dr. Susan, was bent over, peering into the bars of the cat carrier. "No one's at their best when they feel cornered. Why don't we get this sweetheart into an examination room so I can take a look at him?"

Julie took charge of the cat carrier and followed the vet as she led the way into one of two small rooms. This one was decorated in the same fashion as the waiting room, with children's artwork on the walls amid more traditional Christmas décor. The counter along the back wall with drawers of supplies and the stainless-steel examination table were clear of decorations. Julie set the cat carrier on the table and waited for the vet to close the door before she opened the carrier.

Kringle stubbornly did not emerge.

Julie sighed and peered into the carrier. He was huddled near the back, fur standing on end. When she reached her hand into the carrier, he scratched her. "Ouch!"

At least this time, the scratch hadn't broken the skin.

"See?" she muttered under her breath. "Monster."

"You'd be grumpy, too, if you were injured. What did you bring him in for?"

"He's limping. One of his back legs, I think. He didn't let me check."

Susan, in a show of misplaced confidence in Julie's opinion, donned a pair of latex gloves before she reached into the carrier. Maybe the latex gave her some protection, but she was able to coax the cat out, taking some but not all of his weight in her hands until he huddled on the table.

She peered at the cat. "You're one of Myrtle's, aren't you?"

Julie sighed. "Soon. I found him in the Cozy Holly Inn. My family owns it, and I'm here to clean it up before the Christmas Eve party."

Having now said that much, she hoped that Dr. Susan was one of those who had gotten an invitation.

"I heard about that. My dad got an invitation from Ida, and he hasn't stopped talking about it since. He used to be the town veterinarian before he retired, and I took over the clinic."

Everyone in town seemed to pass the family business on. Julie couldn't help but smile. It must be nice, to have a town built on that legacy. Susan very gently examined first Kringle's front legs and then his back legs, cooing to him all the while. Strands of her blond hair fell free from her ponytail, but she didn't seem to notice.

"What's this volunteer thing you were talking about with Nolan?"

"Oh, it's just one of our drives. We have them several times a year. We administer rabies shots to animals in need and take donations for the Pets in Need Fund. We'll have another one for cats around February if this handsome fellow needs his vaccine."

"No, I wasn't talking about Kringle. I was just wondering about the volunteer part."

And, since she wouldn't be here in February, it wouldn't matter. If she wanted to find volunteer opportunities, she could do it in Boston. She hadn't, which probably said a lot about her. Or maybe it said more about Pinecone Falls. There was something about the town that made her want to give back to the community, and she wasn't even a part of it.

Still conducting the examination, Susan said, "We take volunteers to help with the documentation and manage the pets, so they're seen on a first-come, first-serve basis. We always have an influx of patients on drive days. If you're looking to help in February, we'd love to have you."

Julie managed a tight smile. "I don't think I'll be here then."

"Ahh, well, if you are around, keep it in mind." Dr. Susan sighed then straightened. "There's definitely something going on with his left leg. It might only be a sprain, but I'd like to do an X-ray just to be sure."

Julie held her breath and locked gazes with the cat. She could feel her bank account taking figurative coins out of couch cushions to pay for this. Could she afford it?

But how could she leave Kringle in pain? If his leg was broken, he needed it treated properly.

Dr. Susan rounded to her side of the table and put a hand on her arm. "We have payment plans," she said softly. "Or if you can't afford it, we can take from the Pets in Need Fund. It's the entire reason we hold these drives, for emergencies like this when money is tight."

Julie released the breath she was holding. She'd manage to scrape it up. She certainly wasn't going to take the money from someone else who might need it more. "I can pay. It's just that I don't mean to keep him. I'm only in town for a few more days, and he's going to the animal shelter just as soon as Myrtle has an opening. But I don't want him to be in pain or to give Myrtle an unhealthy cat. Do the X-ray."

The vet nodded. She looked at Kringle, considering. "I have an appointment coming in soon, but I don't want to leave you both hanging. I'll sedate him and do the X-rays now, but he'll be a little while coming out of the sedation. We like to monitor the animals to make sure there aren't any adverse reactions. Would you like to go home? I'll call as soon as he's awake and ready to leave."

Kringle's eyes—now a worried sapphire color—caught hers. He seemed to be pleading with her. She couldn't leave. If she did, she'd only worry.

"I'll stay."

Susan smiled warmly. It made her feel like an old friend instead of a customer. "Then let me administer the sedative and hand him off to our vet technician, Stacy. She'll do the X-ray while I talk to you about the various options for painkillers and recovery, depending on what we find."

"But your appointment…"

"They aren't here yet," Susan said firmly. "Let's make the most of the time I have until my next patient arrives."

Julie smiled back at her.

She turned her back while Susan administered the sedative—Julie couldn't stand needles. On the countertop in small frames were photos of past clients and their pets. Julie studied the photos and stopped at one in the center.

She recognized the freckle-faced, suntanned girl holding an oversized tabby in her skinny arms. That was Julie and Whiskers. Her chest ached. She picked up the photo and let nostalgia sweep her away for a cat she hadn't seen in a decade. She'd loved Whiskers with all her heart.

Susan, having left the room, returned every bit as quietly and approached the counter. She looked over Julie's shoulder at the photo. "Remember that?" she asked softly. Clearly, she had recognized Julie this entire time.

She set down the photo amid the others nestled at the back of the counter as if she was a part of this extended pet family. Maybe small-town life had its bright spots, after all.

Her voice thick, she whispered, "Yes, I do."

CHAPTER 19

"Oh no!" Ivy exclaimed. She bent over Kringle, cooing and petting him gently between the shoulders. She and her husband had just arrived at the inn to help cut down the tree. "Is he okay?"

"It's just a sprain," Julie informed her. "As long as he doesn't overexert himself, he should heal in a week or two. The painkillers are helping. He slept like a log last night, didn't even wake me up early for breakfast."

Julie had been relieved to find out the cat didn't need further treatment, but she'd been baffled to discover the bill had been paid. Tina, the receptionist, had mentioned something about the animal shelter paying, but Julie was sure that was a mistake. She'd made a note to straighten that out with the veterinarian later on, but right now she had a more important task to cross off her to-do list.

"Poor thing," Ivy said. The cat lounged on the floor and turned over to show his belly. That was always a dangerous proposition from a cat, especially this one, but the painkillers must have mellowed him out because he didn't try to scratch Ivy when she stroked his belly. He even purred.

Ivy's husband, a heavyset man with a wide smile named Malcolm, shrugged. "She has that way with animals."

"I imagine it's why she decided to open a pet store."

"One of the reasons," Ivy said from where she crouched in front of Kringle. "The other one being that I wanted to do something with my business degree that wasn't soul-sucking. A pet store was the closest thing."

"That," Malcolm said, "and turning our house into a menagerie."

"Are you sure you don't want a cat?" Julie was only half joking.

Malcolm raised his hands. "Please don't encourage her."

Ivy made a face at her husband, but it was all in good fun.

They left Kringle inside and ventured out into the

winter air. The wind was still today, and the sunlight sparkled off a fresh dusting of snow. Some of the footprints she'd left had been filled in entirely; others were now shallow depressions.

"The spot where my grandfather usually cut the trees is toward the back of the property."

Malcolm crossed his arms and looked dubiously at the height of the snowbank. "Am I going to be able to fit my truck out there? I have four-wheel drive, but I've gotten stuck in drifts like these before. It's not pretty."

Julie bit her lip. "Maybe not. I think Gramps always managed by tying the tree to an old sled. It might still be in the shed."

"Let's see the tree first. Then we'll figure out how to get it inside."

Malcolm fetched a chainsaw and some bungee cords from the back of his truck then took up the rear as Julie led the way. She was traipsing through the snow, some places coming up as high as the tops of her boots. On the way, she teased Ivy by telling Malcolm stories of when they were kids. Some of these, Ivy must have told to Malcolm already. But others, he clearly hadn't heard, judging by the way he laughed. By the time they reached the stream, Julie was warm from exertion, from being with friends, and from the nostalgia of simpler times. It shouldn't feel as novel as it did.

"Here," Julie said. It was difficult to tell, what with all the snow and the younger trees popping up, but she thought she'd found the right place. A swath of bare, frozen ground marked where the stream would be in the spring and summer. On her side of the property, the trees were receded a good six feet away from the banks of that stream. On the other side, presumably the Millers' side, the trees hedged in closer. All except for a path leading over the stream on a wood-plank bridge.

She and Ivy argued over which tree to cut while Malcolm tried his best to steer them away from getting something too big. "If we cut a small one, say, no taller than six feet, we can probably manage to drag it back to the inn with or without a sled."

Ivy propped her hands on her hips. "Six feet, Mal? This is going to be *the last* Christmas Eve party at the Cozy Holly Inn. They need a tree bigger than six feet!"

"But maybe one small enough to actually fit in the house?" Julie said gingerly. "The inn has regular ceilings, so anything over eight feet is out. And I need room to put on the tree topper."

"You could always trim off the top branches if it winds up being too tall."

"That sounds like it would make it look weird."

"Well, I don't have a measuring tape. I'm just trying to look out for the best tree!"

After some good-natured bickering, they settled on a tree. It was taller than Julie but not much taller than Malcolm, who was a bit over six feet tall. He marked out where he was going to cut and how the tree would fall and asked them to stand back.

As he started up the chainsaw, someone shouted behind them.

"Hey! Hey, what are you doing?"

Malcolm shut off the chainsaw. In the sudden silence, Julie's ears rang. She and her friends turned to look into the furious faces of two older men. One, Gram's age and moving with slow precision, must be Klaus Miller. His son looked similar, but twenty-five years younger. An older, less-friendly version of Nolan. Julie found herself glancing behind them for Nolan, but he didn't appear.

"What are you doing?" Klaus demanded. He stepped onto the plank bridge, shaking his fist.

"We're cutting down a tree to bring inside. For Christmas?" Julie's voice lost its bravado at the last syllable. She hated confrontation. She fought the urge to bow to shoulders.

"From my property." Klaus stopped in the middle of the plank bridge. Despite his age, he looked formidable. The lines of his face were as severe as his compressed lips.

Julie glanced at this side of the stream. She remembered the plank bridge from her childhood. The trees here had clearly been cut back. "I-I'm sorry," she stammered. "I… I thought this was our property. Gramps used to cut down trees here every year."

"From *my* property," Klaus all but snarled.

"I'm sorry. I… I didn't know. Gramps never said anything about that. We'll cut down from somewhere else."

Nolan's father stood with crossed arms on the far bank of the stream. He looked as angry as Klaus. "The boundaries should have been marked a long time ago."

Klaus took a forbidding step forward. "It doesn't matter. This will *all* be my property in a couple weeks."

It isn't yet. Julie couldn't find her tongue.

Klaus narrowed his eyes. "Unless your grandmother is up to something."

"What? No!"

"Then what is the real reason you're here?"

Julie stood her ground, but it was hard. She hadn't come here to get in the middle of family politics. "Like I told Nolan, I'm here to throw one last Christmas Eve party before the sale of the property. It's the same reason I'm cutting down a tree."

"I bought the property *as is*. Any damage on your part is a violation of the terms."

At that, Julie did take a step back. "What? But… it's a tree." Her voice lacked the conviction of Klaus's. She felt cornered, but she drew herself up anyway. "Gram said—"

Klaus scoffed. "I never trusted Ida with her eternally cheerful nature anyway. If she's trying to break the contract, I won't have it. Now, get off my property."

As much as Julie wanted to argue, she didn't have the will. As she shrank back, Ivy touched her arm. She hadn't gotten in the middle of the problem, and Julie couldn't blame her. They were both ignorant of the terms of whatever sale Gram had arranged. But Ivy did offer her support, and by the time they made it back to the inn, Julie had stopped trembling with the aftermath of nerves.

She shut her eyes and leaned against the door to the inn. "What should I do?"

"I say cut down a tree anyway," Malcolm said.

"But the terms of the sale…" Julie took a deep breath. "I don't want to screw things up for Gram. I'll have to call her."

"Later," Ivy said firmly. "Let's go inside and warm up. Is there some other way we can help today?"

As Ivy led her into the house, Kringle fled. He barely had a limp as he disappeared into the kitchen. But the flash of his white tail reminded Julie that she was home at the inn. She didn't have to deal with Klaus or his son. Not even his grandson, who Julie had actually started to like. If there was one silver lining to today, at least Nolan hadn't been there.

Arms still linked, she and Ivy made their way after the cat to the kitchen. Malcolm followed after. "Are there lights you want strung up along the roof? I can help with that if we're not cutting a tree today."

Ivy smiled at him. "Good idea, honey. Julie?"

Julie shook herself out of her reverie. She pulled herself out of Ivy's hold and turned. "Actually, yes. I have a bin of outdoor lights I've been meaning to put up. There's a ladder in the shed, I think. At least, there should be."

"I'll find it," Malcolm said. "As long as the shed isn't locked."

"It is. Gram locked it up when she locked up the inn. I have a key in the kitchen." As she rummaged through a drawer, she said, "But Ivy, I'd hoped to lure you inside after the tree to help me with something else."

"Oh?"

Julie turned and offered the key to Malcolm. He took it but didn't leave.

She pointed to the heap of bags she'd deposited in the corner earlier that day. "I want to make some party favors. There's going to be a lot of them. I bought wine."

Ivy grinned. "I won't say no to wine."

Malcolm chuckled and kissed the top of Ivy's head. "I guess that's my cue to leave."

"So, what are we making?"

Julie hauled out the bags with the transparent ornaments, paint pens, wrapping paper, and Christmas-themed confetti she'd bought from the nearest ninety-nine-cent store. As she emptied the bags, she explained her idea, and they set to work.

But not without a fortifying glass of wine each.

CHAPTER 20

*N*olan considered himself lucky that he'd even managed to find some vestige of the family's old Christmas decorations, let alone that he hadn't had his dad or Gramps breathing down his neck while he did it. Maybe he should have been more suspicious. The only box of Christmas decorations he'd been able to find had been the ones his mom had loved the best.

Most of these were ornaments for the tree. Crafts that he'd made during elementary school, small little gingerbread figures, the angel tree topper she'd loved so much. Handling each of the carefully wrapped ornaments made his chest ache. He missed his mom on and off during the year, but seeing these ornaments made it particularly hit home that she was gone. When he searched deeper into the box, he found more of her favorite decorations. Little figurines of Santa and reindeer, elves and snowmen, and especially more gingerbread men. These, he pulled out of the box and carried downstairs, arranging them in the public areas.

Gramps came into the room as Nolan was placing the second-to-last one on the mantel alongside a snow globe. His expression, already pinched with anger, darkened. He picked the porcelain gingerbread man up off the end table. "What is this doing out?"

"I put it there."

The words resonated between them. Gramps must have heard the urgency in Nolan's voice because his expression was less angry when he turned to look at Nolan.

Quieter, Nolan said, "They were Mom's."

Gramps didn't look any happier. He didn't put the decoration down, but he gentled his hold on it, almost cradling it to his chest.

Nolan looked at the snowman in his hand and set it down carefully. "The guests have been asking why the house isn't decorated."

"It isn't decorated because we don't *want* to decorate. It's our inn, our choice."

Nolan wanted to tell his grandfather that *he* wanted to decorate. That it would help business but also their mental health. But the pinched look of grief on his grandfather's face stopped him.

Snowball, who had been lounging on the ground by the fireplace, sensed Nolan's mood and shot to her feet. She trotted to him and leaned against his leg. Her support meant something, even if it wouldn't give his argument weight.

Gramps looked around, his expression changing from grief to anger and back again as he looked at the decorations Nolan had put out. "Put them back in the attic." He turned to the next-nearest decoration, a sleigh pulled by reindeer, and grabbed that one too.

"Don't." Nolan swallowed and added, "Please don't."

It didn't seem to help. Gramps pretended not to hear.

Nolan raised his voice. "The guests heard about the Christmas Eve party at the Cozy Holly Inn. They want to know whether we're throwing one too."

"We're not." The two words might as well have been carved from stone, they were as friendly and as immovable.

"I know that, but we have to give them something. A few decorations here and there in the public areas will appease them. It'll bring them back another time. We need repeat customers."

Nolan dropped his hand to the soft fur of Snowball's neck and tried to take strength from her. He rarely argued with his grandfather, but he had to put his foot down sometime, didn't he? He couldn't let his family keep going as they were, nurturing their bitterness and their grief.

"*I* want the decorations." The confession was soft enough he wasn't sure that Gramps heard. He cleared his throat and repeated himself, louder this time. "I want the decorations. They're a little piece of Mom. She might not be here anymore, but she loved Christmas."

Gramps's face softened. He hadn't always been this hard-edged. When Nolan was a kid, Gramps hadn't been able to deny him anything. For a brief second, Nolan saw a glimpse of the old Gramps. The one with the twinkle in his eye and the welcoming expression on his face. There was hope.

"Mary died on Christmas."

"She died after she got to see her favorite time of year one last time. We aren't honoring her by shutting everything away. I think… I think if we brought it all out, if we remembered, we could start to heal."

Gramps stared around the room but couldn't seem to find a safe place to rest his gaze. He looked older all of a sudden. Weary.

"Stan and I found that Green girl chopping down a tree near the stream. On *our* property."

Nolan's first thought was to worry about his grandfather and father out that far in the property in the snow. Trudging through it when there was no clear path was hard work. They could have a heart attack, especially if they hadn't warmed up properly. But then his next thought was more suspicious. Why had they gone out there in the first place? Had they been spying on her?

Pinching the bridge of his nose to stave off a headache, Nolan asked, "What happened?"

"I told you. She was trying to cut down one of our trees."

"By the stream."

"Yes."

Nolan opened his eyes. "You mean the place where her grandparents always cut down the trees?"

Gramps's mouth turned mulish. Nolan wasn't entirely sure the spot in question—he went up that way with Snowball sometimes—was on Gramps's property. "If she crossed into our property, I'm sure it was by accident."

"She's trying to cause trouble."

Nolan wanted to scream. Instead, he counted to five in his head, stroked the top of Snowball's head, and said evenly, "She is not. She is here at Ida's behest, and she's not staying. I've seen proof."

"Then Ida is trying to cause trouble. She doesn't want to go through with the sale."

Nolan wasn't really convinced they needed that property anyway. It would be more to take care of, and they had all they could handle at the lodge. But when Gramps got an idea in his head, it was hard to persuade him otherwise.

"Why not just let Julie cut down one tree? We have plenty on either side of the stream. It's not like she's going to cut down the whole forest."

Gramps turned away with a harrumph. "You can't let those Green women get away with anything." He stomped out of the room, the decoration still in his hands.

Nolan was at his wits' end. He understood his father's and grandfather's need to grieve his mother, but years had gone by. They were poisoning the very memory of her. And it was turning them sour. The old Gramps would have been much more neighborly to Julie. Something had to change for all their sakes. If it didn't, Nolan was afraid he might end up bitter and grouchy like his grandfather.

Maybe he could start with one simple thing. He could do something to make up for his grandfather's Grinch-like reaction to the tree. He could extend the proverbial olive branch.

CHAPTER 21

*J*ulie and Ivy had sipped just enough wine to keep them warm when they moved from the kitchen, where the ornaments with their painted words and numbers were drying, to the porch to string up lights along the banister. Malcolm put up the last string of lights along the rooftop before carefully climbing down the ladder and wrapping his arm around his wife. He looked indulgent, happy. It was a quiet moment that Julie felt strangely on the outside of, despite being on her family's property. The one place, as a kid, where she'd always felt truly at home away from home.

It was so weird to feel envious of another couple. Her friends cycled through boyfriends, some even staying for over a year and becoming more perma-nent fixtures, but those couples never looked like this.

Certainly, Julie herself had never had a relationship that put such a satisfied smile on her face. Maybe it was the country air, so fresh and still. This didn't feel like some quick gesture of affection before rushing to the next item on the schedule. This felt like the bedrock of a relationship.

Maybe Julie had had too much wine. She was feeling overly sentimental.

Ivy looked away from her husband long enough to smirk. "I think that's our cue to leave."

"You don't have to—" Julie started. The inn wasn't equipped for entertaining guests right now, but she didn't want to chase Ivy and her husband away, especially when they'd been so helpful.

Her friend didn't lose that sly look. Instead, she pointed over Julie's shoulder and said to her husband, "Come on, honey. Let's go home."

Julie turned to see a figure emerging from the woods, dragging a pine tree on a sled. It was Nolan.

❄

NOLAN HADN'T REALIZED THAT THIS PROVERBIAL olive branch would be so heavy. It had been a few years since he had chopped down a tree for the house. And, come to think of it, hadn't they often used the sleigh to transport it? He paused at the edge of the tree line and took in the inn standing guard over the clearing.

Julie wasn't alone. There was another truck in the parking lot, and two people on the porch. From the size of one and the riotously curly hair the other sported, he was pretty sure it was Ivy and her husband. Ivy spotted him first and, after hugging Julie, gave him a wave and then tugged her husband toward their vehicle.

Well. That made this a little less awkward. A little, but not much. Nolan took a breath and squared his shoulders.

And almost fell flat on his face when Snowball tackled him. She barked and swerved, coming back for another try, her paws kicking up tufts of snow. He fended her off, laughing, with one forearm.

"I should have kept you in the cone."

She might not understand English, but she knew the word *cone*. Her ears flattened to her skull, and she slinked away warily.

He sighed and held out his hand. "It was an empty threat, and you should know it. If I didn't make you wear it last night, when you were still scratching at the bandage, you know you're safe from it now."

He'd taken the bandage off sometime this morning, showing the pink but healing flesh beneath. The scratch hadn't been too deep, and under his watchful eye, Snowball hadn't made it any worse. Now that she was outside, she didn't even seem to notice the injury.

Nor did she seem the least bit wary of the area where she'd been hurt. She probably would have gone full tilt at the cat too. Luckily, they hadn't spotted any such animals on the way here.

The truck rumbled to life and pulled out of the long drive. Nolan resumed pulling the sled. It was a lot easier once the darn thing was already in motion.

He kept his eyes locked on the inn as he approached. More specifically, on the woman standing on the porch. She was dressed in a thick sweater reaching to mid-thigh over leggings, not a jacket or hat in sight. At least she was wearing boots —and, to his surprise, boots of more sturdy make than the stylish suede ones she'd been wearing when they first met. Her arms were crossed over her chest, not a welcoming sign.

But as he neared the edge of the wraparound porch, she tucked her hair behind her ear and dropped her arms. Maybe she wouldn't condemn him for the way his family had treated her.

He stopped. Out of the corner of his eye, he watched Snowball bounce in and out of snowdrifts, collecting clumps of ice in her fur. He let her play.

He called up to Julie, "I've brought an olive

branch."

"Those have got to be some big olives," she said with a laugh.

The tension in his shoulders drained away. He smiled back. "Imagine the martini glass."

She laughed again. He liked the sound, and the way her eyes lit up from this distance, reflecting the twinkle of the Christmas lights wrapped around the railing.

Don't get too friendly. She wasn't staying in town. He would probably never see her again after Christmas.

And yet, here he was with an enormous Christmas tree. He fiddled with the hat covering his ears. "I heard you needed a tree."

"I do."

Her voice was small.

"How's this one?"

"If you can get it into the house, it's perfect."

He grinned. "That sounds like a challenge."

❄

CHALLENGE WAS AN UNDERSTATEMENT. NOLAN MUST have been superhuman or something because just trying to help him made Julie's arms weak and her back ache. In the end, they had to trim a bit off the bottom in order to stand the tree upright. The one saving grace was the fact that she had already brought down the tree stand in preparation for Ivy's visit.

Once upright, in front of the window and far enough from the fireplace not to be in danger of catching aflame, the tree was a sight to behold. The air smelled fresh with the scent of it. She would have rushed upstairs to get the decorations for the tree if Nolan hadn't reminded her that the branches needed to settle for a day or two. In her apartment in Boston, she only had a small artificial tree, which didn't need the same care.

This, she had to admit, was much better.

"Would you like a cup of coffee?" Julie asked. She and Ivy had finished the wine.

Nolan hesitated a moment before he nodded. "Thanks." His hands were stuffed in his pockets, and his shoulders hunched. He looked slightly out of place.

"You can bring Snowball inside if you'd like." The dog had waited obediently on the porch, her nose pressed to the window, watching them.

Relief flashed across his expression, but he asked, "Are you sure?"

She nodded. "Kringle can stay out of the way if he knows what's good for him." Historically, he hadn't shown that amount of common sense, but she hadn't seen him since she and Nolan had finagled the pine tree into the house.

As she made the coffee in the kitchen, she glanced out at the path the tree had made in the snow. How funny that only hours earlier, his grandfather and father had yelled at her for trying to cut down a tree. And now Nolan had shown up with one. She doubted the older Miller men had had a change of heart, which meant that Nolan had heard about the incident and gone against their wishes to make it right. That said a lot about him.

When she returned, mugs in hand, Nolan had taken Gram's chair. Snowball lay on the floor at his feet, panting happily. She still had a scratch across her nose, but it didn't look bad. The clumps of ice in her fur were an entirely different matter. Nolan was slowly picking them out and turning them into a swiftly melting snowball on his knee.

"Here. I'll get a bowl or something for that." She thrust both cups into his hand and returned to the kitchen. She scouted for the cat—not present—before she found the bowl. The kitchen table and countertop were heaped with the still-drying ornaments. With her luck, Kringle would find his way in here and knock them off and she'd have to start all over again. She and Ivy had chatted while they worked, catching up with a decade of life's gossip, as they painted the words *Cozy Holly Inn* in gold and added small holly sprigs in red and green at the corners. The name on the opposite side of the clear glass ornaments was also in gold with holly berries. When they dried, maybe tonight, Julie would fill them with ribbons of red and green.

She brought the bowl to Nolan, who awkwardly handed a cup of coffee back to her in exchange. Julie took her customary spot on the couch, curling her legs up to one side. She looked at the Christmas tree and smiled.

"Your grandfather told me not to cut down any trees."

"I know."

The two words were clipped. When Julie glanced at him, she found his jaw tensed. He continued to pick at Snowball's fur, even though it looked mostly clean. The dog clearly loved the attention.

"Then why…"

"I'm not my grandfather." Nolan straightened. He still had the coffee cradled in one hand, but he hadn't taken a sip. With the tree blocking a lot of the ambient light from the window, his gaze was shadowed when he turned it to her. "I cut it down from the same area where your grandparents always did."

Julie found it suddenly hard to talk. She took a sip of coffee to ease the tightness in her throat before she whispered, "Thank you." She looked at the tree again, feeling all the more grateful that it was here. If Gram had only one last Christmas in this inn, she wanted it to be the best.

Even if Gramps was no longer with them.

After a minute of silence that turned strained around the edges, Nolan said, "Please don't be too hard on them. Gramps and my dad. They... they have their reasons for being grinches at this time of year."

Julie drew her knees up to her chest and balanced the coffee on top of them. "Oh?"

She watched Nolan take a sip from his mug. His throat bobbed as he swallowed. His hair curled on the bottom edges, wet from sweat or melted snow. He still wore his winter jacket, though it was open. He looked ready to run out the door at any minute.

Strangely, she didn't want him to go. He wasn't like the rest of his family. She genuinely *liked* him.

He said, "My mom... died of cancer a couple years back over Christmas."

She dropped her feet to the floor and set the cup down next to them. On impulse, she reached out to touch the back of his bare hand. His skin was surprisingly warm, given how recently he had been outside. When he looked up, their gazes met and held. She didn't want to move away.

But shouldn't she?

❄

Nolan forgot to breathe when Julie touched the back of his hand. Her touch was gentle, almost hesitant, but it pulled him out of his thoughts. It reminded him that there was someone else here aside from him and more to life than grief.

"I'm sorry," she whispered.

He nodded. He wanted to turn his hand, to lace his fingers with hers, but he was afraid if he tried that, she would pull away. Her cheeks were already high with color, the pink washing out her freckles.

Looking her in the eye, he found nothing but sympathy in her expression. Maybe because of that, he started to speak, to pour out the poison that had been building in him these past few weeks with the approach of another Christmas.

"Gramps and Dad—they're still not over it. It's like they think if they pretend Christmas doesn't exist, maybe they won't feel so hurt. But it doesn't help. They won't let me put up the decorations she used to love. Dad even destroyed all our Christmas photos from over the years."

Julie sucked in a breath. "You're kidding."

Nolan almost wished he was, even if it was no

joking matter. He shook his head. "Mom loved Christmas. It was when she would put the most energy into decorating the house, cooking, baking, everything. She'd sing off-key in the kitchen, with Christmas songs playing in the background." He smiled at the memory.

Julie tightened her hand on his. The movement reminded him of how close they were, and yet how far away. He wished he had chosen to sit on the couch next to her, instead of keeping the arm of the chair between them like a buffer. He wanted her comfort. He wanted...

Something he shouldn't want. He pulled away but offered her a smile so she wouldn't take it personally. "I should get back," he said and stood. He set down the mug and said, "Thanks for the coffee."

He'd barely had a sip. But as much as he wanted to stay, he couldn't. If he did...

No. It was just too dangerous. He knew Julie wasn't staying in town. He couldn't get used to her being here, couldn't turn to her when he needed time away from the stuffy confines of Barrington Lodge. Unlike Gramps and his dad, Nolan was just starting to feel like his old self again after their loss.

The last thing he needed was another broken heart.

CHAPTER 22

*J*ulie had four days to fully prepare for the Christmas Eve party. She must have glanced at her phone a thousand times today. She'd even spent most of the day in the kitchen, finishing up the party favors while taking advantage of the better cell phone signal in here. Kringle had threatened to derail her progress one too many times, but even now he'd tired of the frenetic energy she expended in boxing the ornaments into neat white cardboard boxes and affixing Christmas stickers as a seal, and then cleaning and pacing the kitchen.

Her phone did not ring.

What if Ned Wheatley didn't call in time to fix the sink before the party? The inspection wouldn't go through. All this preparation would have been for nothing.

Worst of all, Gram would be disappointed. All Julie wanted was to make her gram happy this Christmas.

Unable to keep still and having run out of things to do in the kitchen, she retreated upstairs to the attic to fetch down the box of decorations for the tree. She brought them with her into the kitchen and started to sort through them. It gave her something to do.

At the bottom of the bin, she found a photo album. She brushed away strands of tinsel and stray glitter and lifted out the heavy book. She couldn't help but smile. It was exactly the sort of thing she would expect to find from Gram, who still had family photos sent to her by email printed out and placed in an album for safekeeping.

This particular photo album was old. Built like a binder, it was a lurid green color that might once have been pleasing to the eye before age had faded it. On the front was a simple evergreen tree, with words too faded for Julie to make out. When she opened it, she found dozens of yellowed pictures of Christmas Eve parties past spanning several years.

Twin elves, dressed in striped green-and-white tights and matching green tunics. These were young men, not much older than Julie if that, but she thought, if she squinted, she recognized them. It must be Ned and his brother.

On the opposite page was a picture of a much younger Myrtle. Below that, Julie's parents. Her grandparents, holding Julie between them in a red Christmas dress. Gosh, had she ever been that young? She turned more pages, smiling at the faces of her aunts, her cousins, and…

She frowned. "It can't be." The plastic cover of the photo album was translucent with age. She slipped her fingers beneath to pull out the delicate photograph. A man stood, beaming, with his arm around a smiling woman. The woman, Julie remembered only in that vague way of familiarity when too much time had passed. But the man—he, she had seen recently, and he hadn't been smiling.

Julie flipped the photo over to read Gram's inscription on the back. *Stan and Mary Miller.* The date was from twelve years ago.

They could have been two different men, the one in the photo and the grouch she'd met only yesterday. Aside from the shape of the face and the colors of the eyes and hair, they were nothing alike. The Stan she had recently encountered had been grim. The lines in his face had been set in what looked like a permanent frown, not the laugh lines on the man in the photo. He looked a lot like Nolan in the old picture.

She felt for him. Maybe, like Nolan had said, the loss of his wife had wounded Stan deeply.

It had wounded Nolan too. And his father had only made it worse by destroying old memories. This picture didn't have Nolan in it, but Julie kept it out when she returned the photo album to the box, all the same.

Maybe Nolan might want it.

✳

WITH STILL NO PHONE CALL AND NOTHING IN THE house left to clean, Julie decided to take advantage of the day. Before coming to Pinecone Falls, she'd never thought she would have considered a winter day to be beautiful. In Boston, the cold, the slush, even the fresh snow was more like an invasion, a pest to wish away. Not so here.

The temperature had dropped since yesterday. The air smelled clean and fresh. Her breath fogged in front of her face, rising from the scarf she'd wrapped over her nose and mouth. With the sun shining, she didn't mind the chill. The snow was a powder over a layer of ice and more, deeper snow. Each of her footsteps crunched. That steady *crunch, crunch, crunch* was the only thing, aside from the occasional bird call, that ruptured the silence.

She found herself relaxing as she wove in between the evergreen trees. Beneath them, even craning her neck up, she couldn't see the tops dusted with snow. There were too many branches in the way. The pine needles formed a kind of cushion against the rest of the world, making her feel like she was wrapped in a warm blanket. With a woolen hat, mittens, and scarf, and the new boots protecting her feet, she could have walked for hours.

She didn't know where she was headed until she found herself in front of a particularly broad tree. The bark was peeling, the lowest branches over her head. On the trunk, she found her initials. She reached out to run her mitten over the rudimentary letters, and the ones below hers.

The bark of a dog made her jump. She pulled her hand back and glanced in the direction of the sound, only to find Snowball sitting in a drift, wagging her tail and shedding powder into the air that caught the sunlight and sparkled. Nolan stood behind her, a hand on her collar.

He looked chagrined. "Sorry. You looked like you didn't want to be disturbed." He gave his dog a pointed look.

She looked extraordinarily pleased with herself. So much that she stood and strained against

Nolan's hold on her collar in her attempt to reach Julie.

"It's fine," Julie found herself saying. "Let her go."

Snowball bounded up to her immediately. Julie patted the dog on the head, but her gaze strayed to the tree again.

She heard Nolan's steps crunching through the top layer of snow and felt when he stopped next to her. She pointed to the initials carved on the tree. "Gramps and I made those on one of my summer visits."

"I think when you carve your initials into a tree, they're supposed to be next to the boy you like, not your grandfather."

He was close enough to touch. Julie shoved his shoulder, but it was playful. He staggered a step before catching his balance, grinning. Snowball, thinking they were playing, barked and raced off through the trees.

"I was eleven." Despite her defensive tone, Julie was grinning too. It was a happy memory for her, one she'd almost forgotten.

And, since Gram was selling the inn, it was a memory she would once again lose.

No, that wasn't true. Nolan's family was taking over the inn, which must be to expand theirs. She could still book a room with them and come out to the forest to find this tree and remember.

But would it be the same?

"When did he die?" Nolan asked softly.

She glanced up at him. "You don't know?"

He shook his head. "It must have been while I was in school."

"He died just after I graduated high school. It was so rough on Gram."

"Yeah," Nolan said softly. "I get that."

And he did. He was going through the same thing with his mom. Without thinking, Julie reached out and grabbed his hand. It was a bit awkward through their mittens, but she felt his fingers flex beneath hers.

"I'd forgotten that day in the forest until I saw the initials again."

"Oh?"

He was willing to listen. And Julie, for some reason, wanted to talk.

"I was eleven. This was back when I spent every summer at the Cozy Holly Inn. I was always trailing after Gram when she wasn't working. Sometimes even when she was. I think now that maybe Gramps used to take me out for walks just to give Gram some breathing room." She smiled as she spoke. She knew how much they'd both loved her, but she'd also known how much of a little brat she could be. As a kid, she'd been insatiably curious. She raised her free hand to touch Gramps's initials. "That day he asked me what I wanted to be when I grew up."

"And what did you say?"

Chagrined, Julie admitted, "Gram."

He laughed, then at her pointed look, he held up his free hand in surrender. "Look, I can't judge. I'm pretty sure when I was eleven I wanted to be a cowboy."

"But you were such a gawky kid!"

"Is there a law against skinny cowboys?" he asked with a laugh. "And I grew into my height."

At those words, Julie couldn't help but let her gaze skate over his broad shoulders and down his torso. He'd definitely outgrown the gawky phase.

When he cleared his throat, she realized that he'd caught her ogling him. Thank goodness for the cold giving her an excuse for her face to turn red!

"What did your gramps say? When you told him you wanted to be like your gram when you grew up?"

Julie was grateful for the change of topic. She turned her attention back to the tree, more to hide her blush than anything else. "He tried to convince me to be a famous artist like my mom."

"You didn't want that? Sounds pretty glamorous to me."

"No. Mom was always leaving on business trip

after business trip. It's one of the main reasons I stayed here over the summers. I loved her—I still do —but when I was a kid, I wanted... stability? Pinecone Falls was that for me."

"But not anymore?" His voice was low, so hushed that Snowball's frolicking almost overpowered it.

Julie shrugged. "I guess I grew out of it."

"How do you know you didn't grow into it?"

At his words, Julie looked up to meet his eyes. The canopy shadowed them. His cheeks and nose were red from the cold, but he didn't seem to notice. His entire focus was on her. Julie forgot how to breathe.

Just as suddenly as the moment came, it snapped. Nolan tightened his hold on Julie's hand and tugged her away from the tree. "Come with me."

Julie could have protested, but instead, she followed.

❄

WHAT ARE YOU DOING?

Nothing smart.

Nolan should be walking away from Julie right now. If she had once thought she belonged in Pinecone Falls, she'd said herself that she'd outgrown it. It was only his stupid sentimentality, his sense of fairness in wanting to show her something of him after she'd opened up to him in that way.

And he was going to get hurt.

Even knowing that didn't stop him from leading Julie through the silent, watchful evergreens to a clearing not far away from where he'd found her. The line between his family's property and hers was so blurred, he wasn't sure when he crossed over, but the spot he wanted to show her was definitely on Gramps's land. The trees thinned then fell away altogether to reveal an elliptical clearing with a frozen pond in its center. With all the snow, it was difficult to tell where the pond began, or even pick out the large, flat-topped rock by its side. The drifts made the entire clearing all but invisible.

He stopped beneath the trees, still holding Julie's hand. She hadn't tried to pull away once, and he didn't want her to either. "It's a lot prettier to look at in the summer."

"It's still pretty," she said softly. She pointed to a branch. "I think I see a cardinal."

Snowball barked as she barreled into the clearing, tossing up snow. Julie shrieked with laughter and tried to shield herself by tucking herself into Nolan's side. He almost pulled his hand from his grip on hers to wrap it around her shoulders instead.

Almost. The urge was so sudden and visceral, he

found himself raising his arm, but her tight clutch on his hand brought him back to his senses. They weren't dating. He was only here to give her the same consideration, the same vulnerability she'd given him. It was… a peace offering.

The bird flew off from the branch as Snowball jumped headlong into a snowdrift. Julie didn't seem to notice. Her scarf was hanging around her chin and neck, and she was beaming. He liked her smile.

"In the summer," he said, though his voice was pitched low enough not to spoil the moment, "there's a pond here. And a big rock my mom and I used to sit on. When I was a kid, I had a stutter."

"You did not!"

"I did," he insisted. "It mostly came out when I was reading out loud in class. I dreaded being called on. So, Mom would make picnics and take me out here in the summer, and we'd read to each other until the stutter went away."

"Then the reading stopped?" Julie sounded sad. Her face was tipped up to his, the tip of her nose pink with the cold. Her mouth was cherry-red.

He forced himself to look away and shrug. "Not at first. But as a teenager, I thought I had better things to do." Remembering the way he'd brushed her off, he inwardly winced. "I wish I hadn't been such a little idiot."

"I'm sure she loved you, idiot and all."

He snorted. "Yeah. I know she did. I just thought… I thought I'd have more time with her. We started the picnics again after she was diagnosed with cancer, and we moved to Barrington Lodge so we could all look after her on bad days. But she had more bad days than good in the end, and she stopped feeling well enough to make the trip."

He felt Julie's hand tighten, felt the whisper of her words across his exposed skin as she said, "I'm sorry. But I'm glad you have those memories of her, now."

"Yeah." It felt weird, being grateful for a part of his mom that was so far in the past he hardly ever thought of it anymore. "I'm glad I have those memories too."

Gramps and his dad had been so keen on forgetting the bad memories that Nolan had stopped remembering the good ones. He hadn't come to this clearing once since his mom had died. He didn't even know whether the pond was still there or whether it had dried up. It would be a pity if it had dried up.

Maybe, in the spring when the snow had melted, he could come back with a book and read to himself. Or even out loud, even if there was no one to listen. Those picnics with his mom had helped to shape him into the person he was today, and he didn't want to forget about them. He didn't want to forget about her.

"Thank you for showing this to me."

He only wished it was summer, when Julie could have seen it in its full glory. But no, she wouldn't be here come summer. If he came to the clearing again, it would be alone.

Still, he didn't drop her hand, didn't drop that connection between them. He held on to it, on to her, for a few more minutes and murmured, "Thank you for listening."

CHAPTER 23

"*D*on't you dare climb up that tree!"

Kringle was feeling much better today if his boisterousness was any indication. He showed no signs of a limp at all as he jumped up from the base of the tree. Julie lunged to catch him before he clawed his way up the trunk and sent pine needles all over the living room floor. With the agility only a cat could perfect, he twisted to land on the built-in window seat instead. The wide branches blocked her from snatching him off. It was almost as though he was taunting her.

She scowled. "You'd better not ruin the tree. It's the only one I'm likely to get."

Unconcerned, Kringle folded his front paws beneath himself and stared out the window.

The sun hadn't set, but it was moving in that

direction, spreading long fingers of golden-orange light across the snow. Julie had waited as long as she could but now arranged the last boxes of decorations, those due to hang on the tree, by its side. There was something a bit lonely about doing this alone. She decorated her artificial tree alone, of course, but it was a fraction of the size. It took five minutes of her decorating time. And even Julie had to admit, with only herself to impress, she skimped on the decorations.

Not this time. This time, the tree would be as magnificent as she hoped the rest of the house had become. She had so many memories of decorating a tree in exactly this spot with Gram and Gramps.

But she wanted everything to be ready by the time Gram arrived the day before the party. That included making sure the tree was decorated.

Also, she just couldn't wait. She'd run out of other things to clean and decorate, and if she didn't do something, she was going to go crazy waiting for the plumber to call.

As she dug through one of the bins to find a string of lights, the cat on the windowsill made a tittering sound. She straightened and looked out. On the porch rail was a cardinal, preening itself. Kringle made that funny noise again, his attention riveted on the bird.

"I'm not letting you out to terrorize that bird."

Kringle ignored her. The bird ignored him.

Shaking her head, she returned to the box.

This time, when she reached for the lights, Kringle let out a hiss. And then she heard a dog bark. Julie's heartbeat quickened. She peered around the pine branches to see Kringle had arched his back. The frolicking white dog in the yard had chased away the cardinal on the rail.

And where that dog could be found…

Nolan jogged out of the trees, waving his arm as he called for Snowball's attention. She didn't spare him even the briefest of glances but loped up to the porch and pressed her paws against the window.

Kringle was unimpressed.

Julie laughed.

On impulse, she hurried to the front door and yanked it open. She'd swept the snow off the porch, but in her sock feet, she was reluctant to step outside. Instead, she stuck her head out the door and called, "Nolan?"

Her voice came out with more hesitancy than she'd been expecting.

He heard the soft call anyway and jogged from the side of the house toward the stairs. "Sorry," he said with a grimace. "I'll get Snowball out of your way."

"No, that isn't what I—" Julie cut herself off as she wondered just what she had been thinking.

She'd been thinking that it would be much better to decorate the tree with someone else. And Nolan, who didn't have one to decorate, might appreciate it too.

"I'm about to decorate the tree." Julie bit her lip. "I bought hot chocolate and marshmallows if you want to come inside." It was the least she could do since he'd been so kind to cut it down and drag it here.

The smile that lit his face was instant. It chased away the cold winter air making goose bumps on her exposed skin.

"I'd love that."

He sounded as though he meant it.

"Good. Snowball can come inside too. I think Kringle will behave." At least he had last time.

She left the door open as she retreated to the kitchen to make the hot chocolate. Nolan must have taken the time to brush off Snowball's fur outside of the house this time, because by the time he joined her —his outerwear left somewhere else—she was almost finished. She dropped miniature marshmallows into both mugs before handing him one.

Their fingers brushed as he took it. His skin was cold, but for some reason, she didn't want to pull away. She did anyway, tucking her hair behind her ear and leading the way back to the living room.

To her surprise, Kringle had left his sheltered spot in the window. He perched on the arm of Gram's chair, meeting the dog nose to nose. Snowball sniffed him enthusiastically. Kringle kept his claws in this time, even when the dog reached his side and tried to push her snout underneath, nearly unseating him.

Julie laughed. "Would you look at that—they can get along."

"Before you know it, they'll be curled up next to each other in front of the fire."

Snowball tried her best to sniff beneath Kringle's tail. He hissed and jumped off the chair, retreating from the room.

With a wry smile, Julie said, "That might be a daydream. Want to start with the lights?"

Nolan followed eagerly as she led him to the bins with the decorations. She'd removed and tested the lights only a couple days ago, and they lay on the floor in a pile.

"The lights all work?" Nolan asked.

"Yep. Just tested them."

"Okay, I'll straighten them out, and we can get started."

"Good idea." Julie watched as he untangled the loops. "Thanks for bringing the tree, by the way."

"It's the least I could do considering how my family acted." Nolan smiled up at her. "Thank you for inviting me to decorate."

Julie avoided eye contact, pretending to sort through the ornaments. "It's nice to have someone to do this with."

His voice soft, he said, "No, really. You don't know how much this means to me."

She looked up from the bin to find him frowning at the tangled string of lights. He worked methodically to straighten the string out. But his expression had a faraway look that told her he wasn't really paying attention to what he was doing. Snowball sighed and flopped down at his feet, and even that didn't pull him away from wherever his thoughts had led.

"Your family still doesn't want decorations?" she asked.

He looked up. The line of his mouth softened as he nodded. "Yeah. It's always felt wrong not decorating Barrington Lodge. It upsets the guests, but that's not it. Or not all of it. I like Christmas. It reminds me of my mom."

Julie nodded. "I can see that. I'm sorry your family won't budge about the decorations."

The smile he gave her wasn't deep enough to show his dimple. It felt a little sad. "It's fine. But that's why it's nice to be here with you. It feels like I'm actually contributing to the cheer of the season instead of taking it away."

Before she thought better of it, Julie reached out to touch his hand. She didn't look away from his face. "I like that you're here." The tension between them built until, embarrassed, she pulled away. She cleared her throat and cracked a joke. "I'd probably have never untangled those lights without you."

He smiled. Although the air between them was still charged, it was easier to ignore it when she returned to pulling out the ornaments. But with their various confessions, the dynamic between them had changed. It became easier to relax with him, to laugh at the way Snowball chewed on the end of the garland when she unwittingly trailed it across the dog's nose. To chase Kringle away from the box of ornaments before he made off with one. And yes, to tell Nolan about all the small memories contained in each of the ornaments they put on the tree.

Until, at last, there was only one left. The tree topper. When Julie removed it from the box carefully, Nolan got a strange look on his face.

"What is it?"

"Nothing. I've seen that before, that's all."

Julie nodded. "It's the same one that Gram puts

on the tree every year. You probably saw it at one of the parties."

Or in a picture his dad had destroyed. She didn't want to say that out loud, in case it soured the air again.

"Maybe," Nolan said grudgingly. He said nothing else but placed the stepladder in front of the tree for her to climb up. She'd brought it out anticipating having to do all the high branches herself, but Nolan had decorated the ones out of her reach.

When Julie looked down at the delicate angel tree topper, she couldn't help but smile. "This was always my favorite part," she confessed. "When I was a kid, Gramps used to lift me up so I could put the angel on top of the tree myself."

Nolan raised an eyebrow in challenge. "Is that your way of asking me to lift you up?"

She laughed. "No, of course not. I'm not a little kid anymore." But Nolan, with his hands on her waist... that was an image she couldn't shake from her head.

Holding the angel to her stomach with one hand, she climbed the stepladder. Nolan stood on the other side, bracing it so she didn't fall off. His hands on the metal were loose, his attention fixed solely on her. Although she was high enough now, she didn't look away from him. She was taller than him now, for once. And he was close enough to touch. If she leaned forward just a little, he was close enough to kiss.

Woof!

Snowball's bark was followed by Kringle's hiss. And then—pandemonium.

Julie didn't know what had happened. Logically, she knew the dog must have chased the cat toward the tree and the stepladder. But she was thinking this after she'd lost her balance. After Nolan had wrapped his arms around her to keep her from falling.

After she heard a *crash!*

She gripped Nolan's arms, still trying to get her bearings. The cat, she noticed when she looked down, was huddled on top of the wadded-up tree skirt. Snowball was next to Nolan, sniffing him as if wondering what had happened. The stepladder was on its side, though it had thankfully fallen away from the tree, leaving it unharmed.

And the crash? That had been Gram's ornament. Pieces of the angel had been flung halfway across the living room. Julie stared, numb, at the shards.

"I'm so sorry," Nolan said, turning to Snowball and giving her a disapproving look. The dog flattened her ears to her skull and lowered herself to the ground, contrite.

"It's... it's not her fault," Julie heard herself say.

Her voice was a bit distant, barely heard over the thump of her heart. She still didn't let Nolan go, and he didn't try to release her either. "It's just an ornament."

"Right. Just the ornament your grandparents put on the tree every year for as long as you can remember."

Julie shrugged. She pulled away from him, reluctantly. She still felt a little numb, and colder without his arms around her. "I can buy another one. I should clean this up before someone gets hurt."

When she reached for the biggest of the glass shards, Nolan crouched down next to her. His fingers brushed hers and lingered as he gently pulled the sharp piece away. "Let me help," he whispered.

Maybe it was for the best. If she had to do it all herself, she thought she might cry.

The moment on the stepladder when she'd almost reached for him had been wiped clean from her mind in the aftermath.

CHAPTER 24

*J*ulie was getting used to waking up to the quiet sounds of winter in Vermont. The first few nights at the Cozy Holly Inn, she'd woken with a feeling that something wasn't right. No blaring horns, sirens, or traffic. But now she thought the muted silence broken only by the chirp of an occasional bird was much more pleasant.

She had to admit, it was nice to wake up like this. Almost as if she was on vacation.

When she reached for her phone to check the time, she found a text from Ivy.

Ivy: Coffee or lunch today?

She answered an enthusiastic "yes" and crawled out of bed.

Kringle shadowed her steps, pawing at the bathroom door when she stopped at the bathroom before heading down to the kitchen. When she opened it again, he was nowhere to be seen. Downstairs, the sight of the decorated tree—all save for the missing spot on top—caught her attention through the arch to the living room. It hurt, seeing that gap, remembering what had happened to Gram's ornament. An antique like that couldn't be replaced by something she could find at the nearest big-box store. She'd find something, but it wouldn't be the same.

And moaning about it wouldn't piece together Gram's ornament, now shards of glass in the trash. She continued on to the kitchen, only to face the monster responsible for the mishap. The fluffy white cat lay in wait in front of the cabinet housing his food.

Julie needed coffee in the morning if she was even going to approach being human, but she tended to Kringle's needs first. As she cracked open a tin of cat food, she muttered, "Of all the times to pick a fight with the dog, why did you have to choose that one?"

He mewed as she scraped the unappetizing cat food into his dish. He didn't sound sorry, only hungry.

"Well, good luck ruining the rest of the party. You're only here for a few more days at best. In fact, I'm going into town later. I bet a spot has opened up at the shelter. I'll check."

As Julie set the dish down on the floor, a feeling of sadness bubbled up. Surely she wasn't going to miss the ornery cat? Rather than dig into the meal he'd been so anxious she provide, Kringle looked up at her with luminous eyes. He looked a little sad too.

Julie sighed and turned away from him to make her coffee, and when she looked back, he still hadn't touched his food.

The problem was she was starting to get attached to him. She never should have named him. She missed having a cat, and even though Kringle wasn't the friendliest, he was growing on her. He was company. He had no one else. She could kind of relate to that. With her family always so far away, she sometimes felt that she had no one too.

That was silly, though. She had friends in Boston. She had a life there. And her apartment didn't allow pets. She couldn't bring Kringle with her back to Boston, regardless of whether Myrtle had an opening for him at the shelter or not.

As the water for her coffee heated, she reached down to pet Kringle. His fur was soft and warm. He purred beneath her touch and arched to rub his cheek against her hand.

She scratched behind his ears and whispered, "Yeah, you know I'm a big softie. I won't let you get euthanized, even if you are an ornament-breaking little terror."

He started to eat his food, apparently satisfied with the reassurance.

Julie wasn't sure what she was going to do about him. She was still counting on Myrtle to have a spot for him. Or maybe someone at the party would need a new pet. What other choice did she have, to somehow find a reasonably priced apartment in Boston that allowed pets and move there? All while she was technically unemployed?

Right. That didn't sound the least bit feasible.

She went back to making her coffee.

※

SHE WAS FINISHING UP HER SECOND CUP AND LAST night's macaroni and cheese when her phone rang. Hoping it was Ned, she dived for it and fumbled to accept the call. "Hello?" She held her breath, hoping that she sat in the one spot in the house with clear cell phone signal.

"Ms. Green?"

It was a woman's voice. Not the plumber with the parts he needed to fix the sink, then.

"That's me."

The following spiel went in one of Julie's ears and

out the other. She forgot the woman's name instantly —bad for first impressions, Julie!—but the fact that she was calling from the very magazine that Julie hoped to work for drowned out practicality.

"You want me to come for an interview?" she said breathlessly.

The woman on the other line sounded far less impressed. "Yes, we've culled through the résumés, and you're on our callback list. Are you still interested in coming in?"

Julie was in Vermont. She was putting together a party for Gram. She was meeting Ivy for lunch in just over an hour from now. She couldn't just uproot everything and drive into Boston for an interview. But this was her dream job, the best move she could make for her career. So why didn't she feel more excited? Probably because she'd been taken by surprise.

"Sure. Of course. When?" Julie crossed her fingers, hoping the woman would say after Christmas. She couldn't leave with the party planning half done, but maybe she could fly out and zip back and still pull the party together?

"We have a committee coming in the day after Christmas to finalize the interviews. Are you available on the twenty-seventh?"

Julie blew out a breath. That was two days after the party. "Yes. I can make it."

Though, if she had been honest, she hadn't been planning on rushing away *that* quickly. Her family would be here. Gram, Mom, Dad. Possibly a few aunts and cousins. She had to clean up after the party, and it was the Christmas season.

But she'd already answered, and numbly she took the information for her interview. The time, where she needed to be. She jotted it all down on her to-do list before she forgot.

It didn't help. It didn't feel right to bail so soon after the party and leave it to her parents to clean up. She'd have to work doubly hard to get most of it done before she left. She should be excited about this interview, but all she felt was a queasy sort of wish that she had a few more days of vacation before she returned to her real life.

As if sensing her unease, Kringle climbed into her lap for the first time. He rolled himself into a little ball and tucked his nose under his tail, purring.

It helped.

CHAPTER 25

"She isn't staying," Nolan told himself for the twentieth time. This time, it was as he was picking his way through the storage area over the stable. It was the furthest place on the property for Gramps to hide the box of mementos. Nolan, of course, had pretended he hadn't noticed Gramps box up the rest of his mom's Christmas decorations and put them out of sight. But Gramps didn't move as stealthily as he used to.

Up here, the air was cold. The insulation in this part of the barn was nonexistent. It smelled like stale hay, too, with wisps of it crunching underfoot. Nolan had to crouch in order to move through the space without hitting his head. The rafters were low. Mostly, these boxes held old tack. The sorts of things that were too sentimental to throw out, like the halter embroidered with the name of Gramps's favorite horse who had died when Nolan was a teenager. And there, tucked out of sight, was the box of decorations. With a huff, Nolan kneeled to pull the box closer to the flashlight on his phone.

He wasn't stupid enough to take out Mom's decorations a second time. He was lucky Gramps hadn't thrown them all out. But they meant something. They meant just as much as that smelly, faded old halter. Maybe more. And in the box was one particular ornament he needed to find.

Unlike Julie, when Gramps had put up a tree, he and Mary had bickered over whose tree topper to put up. When she'd gotten sick, rather than giving in, Gramps had allowed for a compromise: one year, they would put up the star Gramps liked so much, the next, it would be Mom's angel. The reason Nolan had recognized the angel Julie had pulled from the box hadn't been because of old Christmas photos he'd half-forgotten or a hazy childhood memory of the party. No, he'd seen that very same angel tucked away in the box of his mom's old things.

With gentle precision, he teased the angel out of the box. To his eye, it looked the same. Maybe in slightly better condition than Julie's—she'd confessed that the angel had been handed down in her family, a Christmas heirloom. It had had the scuffed, much-loved look of an heirloom to him. This didn't have the same scratches along the base, and the glass seemed brighter to his eye. His mom had picked this out of an antique shop when he was a kid. She'd loved it, but it didn't mean as much to his family as the one his dog had accidentally broken meant to Julie's.

Still, he didn't get up right away. He held a little piece of his mom in his hands, and he had so few of those left. Julie was going to leave in a few days and forget all about him. He wanted that, didn't he? He had been adamant that he wasn't looking for a relationship.

But there had been that moment in front of the tree with Julie before disaster had struck, and she'd been catapulted into his arms. She was funny. She was warm. She couldn't cook to save her life—even her hot chocolate, which he was pretty sure she'd made out of a packet, had been slightly too sweet. He liked her. He felt he owed her.

No. That wasn't exactly true. He could make amends for Snowball's rowdiness, but that wasn't the reason he was up in the rafters of this freezing-cold barn on the thin planks of wood that served as a floor. He wanted to see Julie smile. He wanted to feel her in his arms again.

He wanted to take a chance. She hadn't left Pinecone Falls yet.

CHAPTER 26

*J*ulie was getting used to people recognizing her and stopping to chat. This time, instead of awkwardly answering their questions in monosyllables and rushing to continue on her way, she stopped long enough to ask their names and after their families, to pass along the news to Gram. She might not remember these people from her summer visits, but Gram had lived all of her life in Pinecone Falls. They were practically family.

She was famished by the time she reached the table Ivy had claimed at the back of the café. Her friend didn't seem to mind the delay but sipped at her coffee and scrolled through her phone while she waited. Julie dropped into the seat across from her with a sigh.

"You couldn't find a table closer to the door?" Julie joked.

Ivy laughed. "You'd only get bombarded by people walking in. You're new in town. Not much happens around here that's new."

With a half shrug, Julie raised her hand to snag Lucy's attention. She didn't even have to look at the menu this time to know what she wanted to order. When Lucy waved back to indicate that she'd seen her, Julie turned back to her friend. "The only interesting thing about me is the party I'm planning."

"Uh-huh." Ivy sounded unconvinced. She leaned her elbows on the table. "And maybe one tall, dark, and handsome neighbor who finds his way onto your property an awful lot…"

Julie had to bite the inside of her cheek to keep from showing her embarrassment. She was still pretty sure she was blushing. "There's nothing between Nolan and me."

Nothing, except for that moment in front of the tree when she'd almost leaned forward and kissed him. Nothing, except for the feel of his arms around her when he'd caught her as she'd fallen. Right. Nothing at all.

But there couldn't be. She didn't do flings, and she was due back in Boston in only a couple more days.

"Right." Ivy drew out the word. She looked like a cat who had learned how to open the cat food tins.

Trying not to fidget, Julie looked away. Lucy was bustling her way toward them, luckily, so she had an excuse. Before the owner of the café reached them, Julie muttered, "There isn't. There can't be. I have a job interview back in Boston on the twenty-seventh."

"What? So soon?" Ivy sounded dismayed.

Lucy was well within earshot by now. "What's soon?"

Although she hadn't been planning on announcing this to the whole town, she couldn't stop the gossip from flying now. It might as well be the right gossip. "I'm leaving for Boston the day after Christmas. I have a job interview at a big magazine there."

Without asking whether or not Julie wanted coffee —she did—Lucy turned over and filled her cup. The aroma of the brew made Julie's stomach grumble. Instant coffee just couldn't compare.

"You have an interview right after Christmas?"

Julie rolled her eyes. "I know. But I want the job. I couldn't tell them to wait a couple more days."

"Well," Lucy said, propping a hand on her hip. "I hope they snatch you up like you deserve. Are you hungry today?"

"Starving," Julie admitted.

After she'd ordered lunch, Lucy retreated to another table. Strangely enough, Julie didn't feel any more excited about the job interview after admitting it out loud. It was happening. She'd been hoping to get this call for weeks. But after all the work she'd been putting in to make Gram's last Christmas at the Cozy Holly Inn a day to remember, the job interview fell flat.

Ivy made a face. "It sucks that you have to leave so soon. I thought you'd be around for a bit after the party."

"I thought so too."

"Will you come back to visit? It's been really nice reconnecting again after so long."

"It has." Julie felt terrible. Her chest felt tight, but she managed not to rub it and give away her unease. "I don't know whether I'll come back. The inn is getting sold."

Ivy nodded. Despite her disappointment, she didn't draw out the moment and make Julie feel even more guilty. She just accepted Julie's decision and moved on. "How are the party preparations coming?"

"I'm almost done, actually. Well, except for the plumbing problem and the inspection. I just want to stop at the ninety-nine-cent store again and grab a few more decorations. Small touches, you know. Something to make the place really shine."

Ivy smiled. She emptied a creamer into the coffee cup that Lucy had refilled. "Anything I can help with? I'll bring the wine this time."

The offer made Julie's throat thick. She'd just admitted that she was leaving in a few days and uncertain whether or not she'd ever see Ivy again, yet her friend was still offering to help. And, despite how little time they'd spent together as adults, Ivy *was* her friend. It was almost as if no years had passed since their childhood days. Ivy was so down-to-earth, so ready to stake her loyalty for friendship. Ivy made time for Julie.

Could Julie really say the same about her friends back in Boston?

"That would be great. I'll pick up the extra decorations today and send you a text?"

Ivy nodded.

Julie gave her a heartfelt smile. "Thanks. It will help keep my mind off of the plumbing disaster."

Lucy arrived with their lunches. This time, Julie had chosen a grilled chicken wrap. It had looked too good last time she'd been here. When she bit into the first mouthful, she knew she had made the right decision.

Ivy wasn't paying nearly as much attention to her

food, maybe because she'd only ordered a pastry and coffee. "Ned still hasn't called?"

Julie shook her head. She held her hand in front of her mouth until she finished chewing. "Do you think I should call him? I don't want to be a pest, but the party is *really* soon."

"I'm sure he hasn't forgotten you. You said he was waiting on some parts?"

Julie nodded.

Ivy shrugged. "Then there's nothing you can do to make them come any faster, except driving to the supplier yourself."

"Trust me, at this point, I'm tempted."

Ivy shook her head with a rueful smile. "Don't worry. The people here won't let you down."

That was the difference between Pinecone Falls and Boston, wasn't it? It wasn't only business to the people in town. It was a community. Ned wanted to help her fix the sink in time for the inspection because he'd be coming to the party too. And maybe he wanted to do it just because it was the Cozy Holly Inn, and it had been there for as long as he could remember, and he knew Gram.

Though it wasn't going to be there for much longer. No, soon it would be an extension of Barrington Lodge. That was if Klaus Miller didn't just have it demolished. That wouldn't make good business sense, would it?

The thought made Julie lose her appetite.

Luckily, Ivy took her thoughts away from that dour turn. "So how have you and Kringle been getting along?"

"Much better since we came back from the vet, actually. I mean, aside from his getting into a fight with Nolan's dog and breaking Gram's favorite ornament."

"Oh no! Will she notice?"

Julie raised her eyebrows at her friend. "It's the one that goes on the top of the tree. She'll notice."

Ivy made a sympathetic face. "I have a spare tree topper at home. I know it won't be the same, but it could do to tide you over for the party."

"That's really sweet. Thank you."

"No problem. Oh! And I forgot. I brought this for Kringle." Ivy dug into her purse and removed a long stick. Tied to the end with a long piece of string was a colorful ball with a feather sticking out. "I thought it might help him warm up to you."

"I'm sure he'll love it." If he had time to play with it. Julie still intended to drop by the animal shelter to see whether a spot had opened up. "But I think the painkillers really mellowed him out. He even sat on my lap this morning. *And* purred!"

Ivy laughed. "I knew he'd warm up to you. He's probably just a bit defensive because he's a stray. You're a cat person, and it shows."

Julie shrugged. "I just hope he opens up as easily with the person who adopts him. I'm going to check and see whether Myrtle has an opening at the shelter."

"Already?" Mouth agape, Ivy looked aghast. "You're just going to dump him off at a shelter earlier than you have to? You still have a couple days in town."

Although her words brought guilt surging to the surface, Julie tried not to show it. "I know, but I don't want him to miss out if there's an opening. And you know I can't get attached, Ivy. I can't keep him."

"I know, but…"

The door to the café opened. As Julie had been doing on instinct every time it had, she glanced in that direction. This time, she actually recognized the person who was coming inside. It was Myrtle.

"Speak of the devil." She waved to the older woman.

With a bright smile, Myrtle waved back. She stopped to say something to Lucy then puttered over to Julie's table. "You look great," she exclaimed. "The fresh air out here is really doing you some good."

Since Julie didn't think she'd changed at all in the

week she'd been here, she sidestepped the compliment with a muttered "Thank you." Then, because small talk was expected, she chatted a bit with Myrtle about her health and about Gram. Finally, when Julie saw an opening, she asked, "So, how's the situation at the animal shelter? Has a spot opened up for Kringle?"

"Kringle?"

Maybe Julie had neglected to mention that she'd named the cat. Oops.

"That's what I'm calling the white fluffball I brought in the other day. I'm only here for a couple more days, so he'll need somewhere to go when I leave town."

"I'm sorry, we're still full up. Unless…"

Julie held up her hands. "No, I know. Don't even say it." She didn't want to think about Kringle or any other cat getting euthanized. "Just let me know whether you get a spot for him." Maybe someone would pick up a shelter cat for a Christmas gift, or Myrtle could find a foster. Worst case, her parents would watch the cat until Myrtle had an opening. They were staying on for a week at the inn.

"I will, I promise. How are the preparations for the party coming along?"

"Almost done," Julie said with a smile. It felt as though she'd completed a mountain of work in the past week, but it would all be worth it when Gram saw what she'd done.

Clearly, Myrtle was thinking the same thing. The expression on her face turned soft, and she said wistfully, "I can't wait for Ida to see it. I haven't seen her in too long."

"She misses you too." Gram had never said as much out loud, but Julie knew from the way she talked about her friends in town that Gram missed Pinecone Falls. It was a shame she wouldn't be able to stay, but they had her situated at a good retirement community right now, somewhere she could be independent but still have access to help if she needed it.

Except, right here in Pinecone Falls there were plenty of folks who would give Gram help if she needed it. But the inn was too much for her to handle on her own. She'd asked Julie to help her run it once… but no, they were past that now. It was being sold, and Julie was interviewing for her dream job. Why had that thought even crept in?

"Do you need any last-minute help?"

Julie exchanged a look with Ivy, who shrugged. "Actually, Ivy is coming over later today after I pick up a few more decorations. Do you want to come put up the finishing touches this afternoon?"

Myrtle beamed. "Absolutely. What time should I be there?"

"When does the store close today?" Julie asked Ivy.

"Five o'clock."

"And the shelter?"

"Before then," Myrtle answered.

"Then, say, five thirty or so?"

Both women nodded. Lucy bustled closer with a white paper bag, which she handed to Myrtle. "There you are, my dear. Did you want anything else?"

"Not today, Lucy, but thank you."

As Myrtle paused to chat with Lucy, Julie wondered whether she should pick up something more than mac and cheese to serve to the two women tonight. They would be coming over close to dinner.

A thread of conversation caught her attention from one table over.

"Storm's going to be a doozy, I hear."

"I sure hope it passes us by!"

"Storm?" Julie asked, surprising herself at her rudeness at interrupting a table of strangers.

"Didn't you hear?" the man asked, not at all taken aback by Julie's question. Julie was surprised at how easily folks chatted between tables here in Pinecone Falls. That never happened in Boston, and it threw her off a bit. "The weatherman is calling for the snowstorm of a century! But don't worry. I hear it's supposed to be south of us."

"South. As in… Boston?"

He shrugged. "Yeah, 'round about there, I'd say."

Julie's stomach plummeted. Her parents were flying in through Boston and meeting Gram there for the drive to Vermont. What would they do if the storm of the century kept Gram away from her last Christmas at Pinecone Falls?

CHAPTER 27

"Don't worry about us," Mom said through the slight crackle of static on the line. Julie was in the kitchen, but she kept stepping in and out of the best pocket of cell phone signal due to her pacing.

"Easier said than done. What if the airport is shut down?"

Dad called over the speaker on her mother's phone, "I'm on hold with the airline now on my phone. We're trying to switch our flight to come into Manchester, New Hampshire instead. It'll be fine."

"Right. And Gram?"

"We're switching her flight too," Mom assured. "Trust me, we're not missing this party."

If anything, that made Julie worry even more. Yes, she'd put a lot of hard work into making sure this party would be one to remember. But if her parents and Gram took chances on the road so they could be here in time...

"Stop fussing," her mom said, even though she hadn't spoken another word. "I swear, you're just like your grandmother."

Julie took that as a compliment. She chewed on her thumbnail. "You have time if there is a storm. You're flying in tomorrow?"

"That's the plan," Dad called. Apparently, the airline still hadn't picked up his call.

"And the party's only the day after that. So, if it's too bad tomorrow..."

"We'll be there," Mom assured. "Now, don't you have other things to do?"

Julie had a pile of shopping bags filled with decorations. Too many, if she was honest. She'd only meant to pick up a couple finishing touches, but she'd been anxious, and when anxious she always managed to spend more than she meant to. At least it would give Ivy and Myrtle plenty to do while they were here. Julie opened her mouth, probably—yes—to fuss, but a beep in her ear informed her of a call coming in on the other line.

"You're right, Mom. Sorry. Keep me updated."

"Love you," her mom said.

"You too!" Julie quickly switched to the other call. "Hello?"

"Well, hello there, Julie." The voice on the other end of the call belonged to Ned Wheatley. "I don't suppose you have a minute for me to swing by? I've got the parts we need to fix that old sink."

Thank goodness!

❋

THIS TIME, JULIE KEPT AN EYE ON KRINGLE WHILE Ned shuffled onto his back beneath the sink. The old man still seemed to think she had adopted a dog rather than a cat, and the very last thing Julie needed was another unexpected vet bill. All the money she was spending on the cat and on buying new decorations to make the party the best it could be was eating away at what little she still had in her bank account.

It wasn't yet two o'clock in the afternoon, so when she heard a knock on the front door, Julie frowned. Ned didn't appear to hear it and was still working away beneath the sink. But she didn't trust the cat, so she scooped him up on her way to answer the door. To her surprise, Kringle allowed it. He even pushed himself higher in her arms to rub his cheek against the underside of her chin.

He must realize that she would be dropping him

off at the animal shelter in a couple days and was mounting a campaign to get her to keep him. "Sorry, buddy, I wish I could keep you," Julie muttered under her breath.

When she opened the door, the cat stiffened in her arms. He clawed his way up her shoulder to jump to the ground, where he huddled behind her legs. But he didn't hiss, which might be an improvement. Well, not for the state of her sweater and her skin beneath.

The man on the other side offered her a sheepish smile. He had one hand on his dog's collar, not that Snowball seemed to notice. She leaned forward, putting her entire weight into reaching Julie and sniffing the cat through the gap in her legs.

"Sorry," Nolan said. "I didn't realize you'd be holding the cat."

"It's fine. At least they're not fighting."

Not a hiss, not a growl. Kringle even endured Snowball's nose, wet and cold with snow. Just in case one of them decided to bolt, Julie stepped to the side. She didn't want to get caught in the middle.

"Do you want to come inside? It's freezing out today."

Nolan shrugged. "It's not so bad." But he stepped into the house and pulled the hat off his head. "I'll only stay for a minute. I brought you something."

Snowball advanced until she backed Kringle against the wall, giving him a vigorous once-over. Sitting back on his hind legs, Kringle batted her on the nose, but he hadn't unsheathed his claws. Progress.

Julie turned her entire attention on Nolan. "You did?"

With a nod, he pulled something wrapped in yellowed tissue paper out of his pocket. She took it, feeling the hard planes of glass and maybe wire in the figure hidden beneath.

"To replace the one we broke."

He'd brought her a tree topper. "You didn't have to. You didn't break it. It was an accident."

"It was my dog that caused the accident."

With a wry smile, Julie shook her head. "It takes two. Kringle is no saint. But thank you. That's very sweet. Do you want to stay for a cup of coffee?"

"I'll stay for a minute or two, but I don't need the coffee. Maybe we can finish what we started?"

Julie hadn't realized how close they were standing until he said those words. He still had most of his outerwear on, his hair a tousled mess from the hat. His smile made her stomach flip.

Finish what we started. They'd stood close like this on the ladder just before disaster had struck. She'd been leaning closer, thinking about kissing him. He was close enough to kiss now, and he wasn't pulling away...

He cleared his throat. "With the ornament? I don't like to leave a job unfinished."

Right. The ornament. He wasn't talking about kissing her at all.

Julie's cheeks flamed. She turned her back to hide it and said, "Right. That's a good idea. Let me get the stepladder."

He took a minute in the entryway to remove his boots and coat. That gave her the time she needed to get herself under control. Yes, Nolan was attractive. Yes, he was sweet and thoughtful. But she was leaving in only a couple days, so there was no future.

She had the stepladder all set up by the time Nolan joined her in the living room. Snowball trotted in after him with a curious white cat lingering in her shadow. Julie snatched up the still-wrapped ornament from where she'd set it down on Gramps's rocker, just in case the two animals got rowdy again. Although she felt a bit self-conscious with Nolan watching her, she carefully unwrapped the gift.

And forgot how to breathe. There it was, in all its finely wrought glory. The delicate wings, the elegant shape of the angel with head bowed as though in prayer. Julie traced the shape of the ornament, the identical twin to the one that had broken.

With tears blurring her vision, she looked up at Nolan and whispered, "Where did you find it?" Her voice almost broke.

He gave a one-shouldered shrug as if the answer didn't matter. "We had it in storage. Remember how I said I recognized it?"

"It was your family's? This belongs to—" Instinctively, she held her hands out with the ornament between them.

Nolan shook his head and raised one palm. "It belongs to you. My family doesn't decorate anymore. It means so much more to you."

She couldn't argue with that. Instead, she stepped into his embrace and hugged him, careful to keep the ornament where it wouldn't be crushed. He hesitated a moment before his arms encircled her. His aftershave was no more than a light, teasing hint of spice and pine. He was warm despite his time outdoors. Solid. She couldn't find the words to thank him, but tucked into his chest, she didn't feel the need to fight for those words. He understood. It was why he'd given her the ornament to begin with.

When she stirred and started to pull away, he let her go immediately. She lingered, not wanting to step out of his protective circle. But she was being mushy and sentimental, and as much as she wanted to kiss him right now, in this moment, he hadn't given her any clue that he wanted to do the same thing. So, she stepped away and approached the stepladder.

At the base, she glared at the two animals, currently curled up on separate ends of the room. "No funny business this time." Her voice was still a little hoarse with emotion, but Nolan didn't mention it.

He chuckled and stepped forward to steady the ladder. "Ready?"

She nodded. It felt almost anticlimactic to place the angel on top of the tree without the animals throwing a ruckus. But as she stepped down, off the ladder, and looked up at her handiwork, she choked up.

"Now it's perfect."

Nolan didn't argue with her. He just laid his hand over hers, where it still gripped the rail of the stepladder. She didn't pull away.

As the silence between them lengthened, she remembered she had something she'd been meaning to give him as well. She only hoped it would mean as much as what he'd given her—a Christmas miracle.

"I have something for you too."

When she started to move away, he caught her hand. "You don't have to. I didn't bring you the angel hoping for a gift in return."

"I know. I had this for you anyway. Wait here, I'll go get it."

She slipped from the room before he could protest.

When she'd removed the Christmas photo of his parents from the album, she'd put it in a drawer in the kitchen for safekeeping. It didn't take her long to retrieve it.

While she was there, Ned pulled his head out from under the sink. "There we are. It was a good thing I came today in case I needed another part and the storm held up delivery. But you should pass inspection with flying colors."

Julie was too distracted by Nolan waiting in her living room to even feel relieved at that news. "That's great. So, you're all done?"

"Yes. Just cleaning up, and I'll be on my way out."

"Great. I hope you don't mind, but I left Nolan in the living room—"

The old man cracked a smile. "The Miller boy is here, is he? Give him my best. I haven't seen his grandpop for months! I wonder how that old bear is getting on."

Of course he knew Nolan. In Pinecone Falls, everyone knew everyone else. But the look of pure joy Ned wore reminded Julie of all the benefits there were to a tight-knit community. When everyone knew everyone else, everyone also cared about everyone else.

"I'll pass along the message."

When she returned to the living room, she found Nolan perched on the edge of the rocker with Kringle in his lap and Snowball doing her best to displace him. Nolan looked up when she laughed.

"You look popular."

The corner of his mouth raised in a wry smirk. "I can't pay attention to another living creature without Snowball wanting in on it."

He gave the cat one more stroke along his back before standing and placing Kringle on the chair. Kringle immediately vacated it, causing a small scuffle when Snowball tried simultaneously to follow him and put herself in between him and Nolan. She was certainly a jealous dog, though she hadn't seemed to mind when Julie had been that close to Nolan.

"Ned's in the kitchen. He says hi to you and your grandfather."

Nolan nodded as if expecting that. "I saw his truck out front. I hope I didn't interrupt…"

"You didn't," she said quickly. She moved close enough to hand him the photo. "It's not as nicely wrapped as the gift you gave me, but here. I found this and thought you might want it."

When Nolan looked at the photo, his smile slipped. "That's my mom."

Julie tucked her hands in the pockets of her jeans. "She and your dad must have come to one of Gram's Christmas Eve parties. I found that picture in an old album."

Nolan grazed his thumb along the edge of the photograph. He said nothing. Maybe he couldn't. When he looked up, she thought she noticed unshed tears in his eyes.

"Thank you. I… I really can't thank you enough. I have to go give this to my dad. Maybe it'll be what he needs to help him realize that memories of Mom are happy ones, not to be avoided. He was hurting when he threw out those old photos. But this…" Nolan carefully held the photo to his chest with one hand. "This could change everything."

Julie opened her mouth, but before she could say anything in response, he swept her up in a hug. It was every bit as fierce as the one she'd given him earlier. Maybe more so. She hugged him back until he pulled away.

He was already sidling toward the door. Snowball, sensing the change, was on her feet and following after him. "I'm sorry to just up and leave like this…"

Julie waved him off. "Go."

He left her smiling. She still felt the echo of Nolan's arms around her.

And a small part of her couldn't help but wonder if maybe Stan wasn't the only person in for a change this holiday season.

CHAPTER 28

 $\mathcal{S}$ tan liked to keep busy at this time of year, as evidenced by the fact that Nolan found him hefting a pail of cleaning supplies after cleaning one of the client bathrooms. They hired a woman to do the cleaning for them. She must be on holiday— grinches though they were, Gramps and his dad didn't deprive anyone of their vacation days.

Seeing Nolan, his dad stopped in his tracks and grunted. "Wanna give me a hand?" Stan wouldn't admit it, but age was creeping up on him, too, especially in his hands, which had developed arthritis.

Nolan took the pail. "Do you have a minute? I want to show you something."

"Sure. I could use a coffee break anyway." Stan led the way to the kitchen, but Nolan stopped him just before the door.

"Wait. I have something for you."

Stan paused in the doorway. Snowball, the traitor, was lounging on the tiles in front of the oven. Nolan had a chicken roasting in there that he should baste soon. When his dad turned to him, he put all thoughts of supper from his mind and instead gently removed the picture from his shirt pocket. He'd been careful not to crease it on the way home. Holding it, he could still smell a whiff of Julie's strawberry shampoo.

Or maybe that smell was clinging to him. He *had* hugged her, after all. Twice. The first time, he couldn't take credit for. She'd been so moved that he hadn't been able to turn her away. But the second?

Don't get attached.

Too late.

He knew there could be no future with her, but the feel of her in his arms had been worth the future pain he'd feel when she left. How far was Boston from here? Maybe they could manage something long-distance…

Stan cleared his throat.

Feeling the heat climb into his cheeks, Nolan looked down at the picture cupped in his palm. His mom looked so happy. It would kill him if Stan ripped this one up. It might be the last Christmas photo he would ever have of her.

He held it out to his dad, lump in his throat, and said thickly, "Please don't destroy this one."

Stan took the photo.

For a full minute, he didn't say a word. His lips were pressed tight together. His Adam's apple bobbed as he swallowed. When he looked up, tears were gathered in the corners of his eyes, not that a man like his dad would ever admit it.

"Where did you get this?"

"Julie Green. She found it in one of the photo albums in the inn." Nolan hesitated then ventured, "I didn't remember that you and Mom went to any of the Cozy Holly Inn parties. I thought Gramps didn't like Ida."

The tension in Stan's mouth went away. His mouth curved into a wistful smile. "You know your mom. She couldn't pass up a Christmas party, and she loved everyone no matter what your grandfather's feelings were. I swear we went to every single party thrown by any of her coworkers. And yes, the Cozy Holly Inn too. I remember this."

Gently, Stan swiped his thumb over the photograph. When Stan looked up from the photo, it was like he was seeing their barren kitchen for the first time. "Gosh, she'd hate this place."

When his mom had been alive, the kitchen had been filled with decorations at the holidays. Mats with reindeer on them. Dish towels with little elves. Plates and glasses with holly stamped around the rim. They had none of that, now.

Stan tottered over to the counter as though unsteady, but his hand didn't shake as he made not one but two cups of coffee. He hesitated then rummaged in the cupboard until he found the cinnamon. He shook some on top of both cups and handed one to Nolan.

"Your mother used to like to spice up her coffee at this time of year."

Nolan hadn't been a kid when his mom had died. He knew this. He'd made her coffees exactly like this one, but with too much creamer. "Yeah, but she also liked that disgusting eggnog-flavored creamer. Do you remember?"

Stan laughed. He actually *laughed*. Nolan couldn't remember whether he'd seen his dad laugh in the years since Mom had passed. Nolan laughed with him, feeling the constriction in his chest start to dissipate. Maybe they would finally begin to heal as a family and move on.

He revised his hopes when Gramps marched into the kitchen with a dark look on his face. "What's so funny in here?"

Nolan's chest constricted again.

To his surprise, his dad answered the question.

"Do you remember that creamer we used to get for Mary around Christmastime? The eggnog one?"

Nolan held his breath.

The crease in between Gramps's eyebrows deepened before smoothing out altogether as his expression relaxed. "That awful stuff? Al Henderson had to order it in special for her since no one else in town was fool enough to drink it. Don't tell me you miss it!"

"No," Stan assured, one hand raised. A smile still pulled his cheeks tight. It was an unfamiliar expression on him since his hair had started to recede so badly and he'd gained more wrinkles. It reminded Nolan of the man in the picture on the table.

The old man shuffled closer and sniffed the air. "What's that you've got?"

"Just a little cinnamon in with our coffee, like Mary used to make it."

Nolan volunteered, "I can make you a cup."

"Don't be silly. I still have half a cup of coffee right here."

And goodness only knew how old it was.

Nolan unfolded from the table. "It's no trouble."

He reached for Gramps's cup, but the old man pulled it away. "No sense in wasting it. I'll just add a shake of cinnamon on top and reheat it."

It was probably that cup's fifth time in the microwave today, but Nolan was too shocked to protest further. He sat again as Gramps puttered around the kitchen fixing his coffee.

Stan said, "Remember that one party your mom had us throw for the kids in your class? The cookie-decorating party?"

When Nolan slowly let out a breath, it whistled through his front teeth. "Oh, I remember. Mom had me dress up as an elf and help. I was not nearly young enough for my friends at school to think that was cute."

Stan guffawed at the memory. Even Nolan spoke of it with a more rueful resignation than anything else. His memories of the teasing he'd received after-ward had faded, and all he could remember was his mom's excitement as she put on her Mrs. Claus costume. This, after she'd taken up his entire Saturday baking the sugar cookies and gingerbread cookies with her.

With a grunt, Gramps lowered himself into his customary chair at the table. He glanced at the picture. His expression softened. "I remember that party. She had me dress up as Santa and bring in candy canes for everyone."

Nolan leaned back in his chair. Gramps wasn't smiling—he was far too stoic for that—but he wasn't scowling either. Maybe this was a good sign. Keeping his voice casual, Nolan asked, "Why was that, anyway? She was Mrs. Claus. Shouldn't Dad have been Santa?"

"That's what I said," Stan grumbled, but he had a smile on his face when he said it. "Your mom said I was too young to be a convincing Santa. So, she stuffed me into that elf costume too. I think she just wanted to see us matching in the pictures."

The smile fell off of Stan's face. Inwardly, Nolan cursed. There it was, the reminder that Mom was gone. Nolan tensed, expecting the same dark mood to come over the table.

Instead, his dad said, "Maybe one of your cousins still has a copy."

"I bet Martha does," Gramps said slowly, warming to the subject. "You know how she hoards photos, especially the ones that she gets in Christmas cards. She always said she likes to see how everyone turned out."

"Did we get a Christmas card from her this year?" Stan asked.

Gramps hesitated. "I think I already threw it out."

Silence enveloped the table, punctuated only by Snowball's whine as she begged for the food cooking in the oven. Nolan ignored her.

He said, "I have Martha on Facebook. I can ask her if she still has any old Christmas photos. She could send them to us digitally."

The disappointment on his dad's face lifted. "Yeah? Maybe that Facebook is good for something, after all."

To Nolan's surprise, Gramps said, "A few of the guests have been asking about Christmas decorations."

"Do we still have any?"

Nolan's throat constricted. Had Gramps thrown out the box he'd found?

But the old man nodded. "Some of Mary's old things. Not all, mind. But enough. When you put some out the other day, it got me thinking… maybe it is time we at least made a show of celebrating the holiday."

"I could pick up a few more things in town. If you're interested in decorating this year. We still have time." Only a couple days before Christmas, but that would be enough. He held his breath and waited.

Gramps and his dad exchanged a look. Then, ever so slowly, Gramps reached out and tugged the photo of Nolan's mom and dad closer. His lips curled in a smile. "Only buy the things your mom would have liked."

That didn't narrow down the offerings by much, given how much she adored the season.

Gramps said, "Maybe we should clean up the old sleigh too. People hereabouts might like to go on a sleigh ride, and goodness knows those horses could use the exercise."

Nolan's mom had been the last person to use that sleigh. The entire family had bundled in with her, with Stan driving. It had been magical. But then, it had been magical every year. Sleigh rides, and then indoors again for hot cocoa in front of the fireplace. But what would his dad say to someone else using that sleigh?

Stan nodded. "Yeah. Especially the kids around here. I bet they'd get a kick out of it. You sure did, growing up. I used to have you in the driver's seat next to me."

"I remember."

Squinting, Gramps turned to pin Nolan with his stare. "Speaking of kids, when are you going to give us a new baby around here to spoil?"

Oh, boy, what in the world had gotten into his grandfather? "I'm not even dating anyone, Gramps."

"You're not getting any younger. And neither am I. You're going to let life pass you right by if you're not careful."

Stan suggested, "Ida is throwing one of her Christmas parties. Maybe we should throw one here too. It would bring all the local girls around, and you never know what might happen under mistletoe."

When Gramps looked like he might be considering the idea, Nolan groaned. "Please don't. I mean, we can't. There's no time to plan a party."

The two other men deflated a bit. "Yeah, I suppose you're right."

Silence. Nolan cast around for another memory to lighten the mood but couldn't think of one. Instead, still preoccupied with Julie, he blurted, "The Cozy Holly Inn is coming along nicely. Julie has it all decked out. All she needs now is for it to pass inspection." Remembering something Gramps had said a couple days before, Nolan added, "Gramps, didn't you mention that you were going to do a favor for the inspector? Maybe you could put in a good word for Julie while you're at it."

Klaus shifted guiltily in his chair. His open expression closed off again as he turned to look out the window, at the snow-dusted trees and boiling gray clouds behind them. "I... ahem. That... might not be possible."

Without asking, Nolan knew that his grandfather had done something. Something that might ruin all the plans Julie had been working toward this entire time. Despite the sick feeling in his stomach, he had to ask. He had to know.

"Gramps... what did you do?"

His grandfather pressed his lips together tight and didn't answer.

CHAPTER 29

*L*ooking at her handiwork, Julie couldn't remember a time when she'd felt so satisfied.

Admittedly, the hot chocolate she, Ivy, and Myrtle were drinking helped with that feeling of warmth. But the inn itself, sparkling around her with twinkle lights and festooned with Christmas decorations, created a cozy feeling in and of itself. Julie didn't want to leave.

She drained the last of her hot chocolate and fished out the marshmallows that had fallen to the bottom of the cup. "I think we're done. Thank you so much for coming over to help, both of you."

With pursed lips, Myrtle shook her head. She wore the kind of ugly Christmas sweater Julie wouldn't be caught dead in, but on her, it looked cute rather than corny. "It needs one more thing—mistle-toe. Ida always hung a sprig in the doorway to the kitchen."

"I still have tomorrow. I can run into town and pick some up then."

"No, no. Don't be silly. I have some in the car. I'll just go get it. Just be sure Kringle doesn't get into it—it's poisonous for cats. I also have a toy out there that I forgot to bring in for him."

Julie looked ruefully at the cat. He was spread out over the new snowflake-printed rug she'd laid out in front of the fireplace, batting around a toy mouse wearing a Santa hat that Ivy had brought. Her friend had brought a matching Santa hat for Kringle, but the cat had resolutely refused to wear it. Julie had to admit, the picture she'd taken of his grumpy face with the hat sliding over his ears was adorable. It was now the lock screen on her phone.

"Thank you for thinking of him, but I don't think he needs any more toys, Myrtle. He's going to be with you in a day or two. Will I be able to drop his toys off with him when I leave him at the shelter?"

Kringle caught the mouse in his teeth and bit down hard. He seemed to be looking directly at her while he did it.

"Don't be too hasty," Myrtle said as she retreated to the door. "You never know what might happen."

"I'm leaving the day after Christmas so I can be back in Boston in time for my job interview. He doesn't have a lot of time left, though maybe my folks could keep him here another day or two."

Myrtle didn't listen to her protests. She was already out the door. Julie sighed.

Ivy crouched in front of the cat, tugging at the mouse's tail as she played with Kringle. "It really is a shame my husband is allergic. Kringle is a sweetheart."

Julie showed her friend the grumpy face of the cat on her phone screen. Ivy laughed. But she didn't argue. That face was proof enough. Kringle was only sweet when he wanted to be, which wasn't often. More often he was a little terror.

But she liked him anyway. He had personality.

Myrtle popped back into the house with an elaborate donut-shaped toy with a ball inside. "Just a little something," she murmured as she placed the toy next to the cat on the rug. Kringle sniffed it but was too attached to the mouse Ivy was trying to get away from him to play with it.

With a satisfied smile, Myrtle rose. "Now, shall we put up the finishing touch?"

❄

Julie fell asleep that night warm in the bed she was starting to think of as her own. Kringle took up most of the pillow, his soft fur brushing her nose and his purr lulling her to sleep. She left the curtains on the window open, hoping to look out at the patchwork of stars. Unfortunately, with all the clouds in the sky, she couldn't even see the moon. But there were lights in the distance, broken up by the silhouettes of the trees. The lights of Barrington Lodge.

Had Nolan given his dad the photo? Julie fell asleep wondering whether the exchange had gone well, whether Nolan had finally been able to get through to Stan.

She forgot the question by morning. Mostly because she woke to Kringle batting at her face with his soft paws. Early-morning light streamed through the window, a gray light that matched the cloud cover. A bird swooped across the window frame and out of sight again, its chirp echoing in the morning. With a groan, she got herself out of bed.

"All right, all right. I'll feed you."

Kringle was sitting by his cupboard door by the time she made it down to the kitchen, looking grumpy at having to wait.

"I'd be grateful if I were you. I could put that Santa hat back on you instead."

He gave her a scornful look. Then again, his face usually looked like that. Smiling to herself, she opened one of the last few cans in the cupboard. She'd bought more cat food than she'd needed to. After all, today was the twenty-third of December. Her family was arriving today. The party was tomorrow. She'd be leaving soon after, and Kringle would be going to the shelter and, hopefully, another home.

She shouldn't feel so sad that she wouldn't be feeding Kringle for that much longer. After all, she liked sleeping in. But his new owners would have to learn his preferences all over again. Maybe she could make a list, to tell them things like how he liked the salmon-flavored food but not the turkey.

He gobbled down his morning salmon while she made her cup of coffee. As she sat at the kitchen table, watching him turn his nose up at the food that had somehow touched the edges of the dish, leaving a hole in the middle where he'd eaten, she shook her head. Cats could be so wonderfully finicky.

"I'm going to throw the rest of that in the trash if you don't eat it." He never touched the food after it had been out for a few hours. She couldn't much blame him for that, but cat food was unappetizing to her to begin with. She didn't even like canned tuna meant for human consumption.

Instead of leaving her to her business and trotting off, Kringle cleaned his face and then prowled closer to rub against her legs. He must sense how close she was to leaving if he was sucking up this bad. She liked it anyway.

"Let's see what we have to do today." She opened her to-do app and checked the contents of her list for the day. Although she'd prepared the inn from top to bottom, today she had to make sure everything was perfect. The first item on the list was to double-check that the rooms she'd prepared for Gram and her parents had stayed as neat as she had made them. Who knew what destructive behavior Kringle got up to when he was out of sight.

"All right, furball. Let's go check the rooms."

To her surprise, he followed as she carried her coffee back up the stairs to the second floor. Everything on the ground floor was spotless, from the table in the dining room she'd finally set up, now that more people than only her would be here, to the hallway that she'd decorated with garlands and snowflakes. Kringle hadn't decimated the Christmas tree. He met her on the second floor, lounging on the floor in front of her as if he hadn't a care in the world.

When she tried to step over him, he attacked her feet.

"None of that, you! We're working."

Kringle, on the other hand, was playing. He refused to move from the center of her bed as she stopped in to make it, wanting every room to look as properly made up. There was something soothing about the uniformity of each of the rooms. Although the bedspreads were different and she'd put out different snow globes and figurines in each to help add to the Christmas cheer, each room was laid out the same way. Bed, dresser, small TV, window overlooking the trees. She checked underneath each bed to make sure Kringle hadn't batted something underneath, and other than getting a face full of fur when Kringle met her halfway, she didn't find anything.

She grabbed for him, and he dodged away playfully. She laughed. "You're in a good mood this morning. Well, don't get too excited. I still have plenty to do. I'm sure Mom, Dad, and Gram won't want to eat mac and cheese, so I'll have to go into town for some groceries. And I have to be back in time for the inspector. He's due to arrive just before they do. So I can't stay frolicking with you all day."

Undaunted, Kringle chased her as she left the rooms, carefully closing each door behind her. It felt normal to walk down those stairs to the first floor, to catch a glimpse of the living room on her way to the kitchen to deposit her empty mug. The snow-covered trees, the cat running past her and lying in wait—it all felt normal. Like home. Her chest tightened as she rinsed out her coffee mug and put it aside. Kringle had taken up a post in front of his cabinet door, the rascal.

"I can't stay." Maybe if she repeated it out loud, that would make it feel more real. The problem was that all of her best memories were in this house, with Gram and Gramps. Again, but with far less conviction, she murmured, "I can't stay."

Or could she? Could she step into Gram's shoes and run this place? She didn't know the first thing about running an inn. But Gram was still alive, and if she came back to the inn to give Julie a little guidance…

No. No, it was a ridiculous thought. "Gram's selling this place to Klaus Miller," Julie informed the cat. He looked unimpressed. "And I have my life back in Boston."

A life, admittedly, that she hadn't thought a lot about these past few days. When was the last time she'd texted Cheryl? She'd been so focused on getting the inn up to shape that she hadn't even had time to prepare for her impending job interview. The excitement that she'd expected about the prospect of a new job had never set in. Instead, she'd been spending time with Nolan and Ivy, with Myrtle and Kringle.

"I have to go," she said out loud again. Kringle tilted his head and gave her a curious look. She couldn't blame him. Even she could hear the lack of conviction in her voice.

CHAPTER 30

*O*ne benefit to having a friend who owned the local pet store was that Julie could stop in at any time and chat. She checked her phone before she went in and decided she had at least fifteen minutes before she had to head back to the inn to wait for the inspector. With the cold weather the way it was, her groceries would last more than that amount of time in the cab of her rented truck.

The store wasn't empty when Julie walked in through the door. An old man was paying for a bag of dog food. He stopped to ask after the party.

Julie gave him a bright smile. "We're all ready to go. I'm just waiting for my gram to get in now."

"It's been some time since I've had a chat with Ida. I look forward to seeing her at the party."

Julie nodded and extricated herself. With half an

ear, she listened as Ivy finished up the payment and offered to carry the bag of dog food out to the man's car. Julie found herself in front of the cat treats, almost as if Kringle had planted the idea in her mind. But it was Christmas, wasn't it? She picked up a bag of festive cat treats and a tin of cat food that Kringle hadn't tried yet. A Christmas treat.

Ivy laughed when Julie laid the items on the counter. "Are you sure you aren't keeping that cat?"

"Just a few treats for the holiday before we have to part ways." The thought made Julie sadder than she imagined.

Her friend bagged the items efficiently. "I'm just saying, he's going to be spoiled and not used to slumming it when he moves on to the next family who adopts him."

"I'm sure he'll grow on them. He did on me."

Ivy rolled her eyes as Julie tapped her credit card to pay. "Yeah, but underneath all those too-fashionable-to-be-practical clothes, you're a crazy cat lady at heart."

"Hey! What's wrong with my clothes?"

"Nothing. I'm just saying they're not doing much to hide the 'I Heart Cats' T-shirt you're hiding underneath them."

If her friend had been standing any closer, Julie

would have shoved at her. Playfully, of course. Mostly. She prided herself on the way she dressed.

When her phone chimed in her coat pocket, she almost jumped out of her skin. The cell phone signal was so shoddy around here that she'd gotten used to not hearing it. Apparently, in Pinecone Falls itself, the reception was better than at the inn.

She fished out the phone. "It's the inspector."

"Ted?" Ivy asked.

Julie nodded. She answered the phone.

The longer his voice rang in her ear, the more hyperaware she was of everything around her. The smooth feel of the plastic bag in her left hand. The blast of cold air and tinkle of a bell as someone stepped into the store. Ivy's assurance that the package was waiting just right here behind the counter. The spring in Ivy's curls as she bent to retrieve a case of cat food.

"That's... you have to be kidding me." Even Julie's own voice sounded foreign to her ears.

Ted, on the other hand, sounded apologetic. "I'm sorry. I had no idea that the storm was going to blow in. There's no way I can get out of Boston today. Maybe not for the next few days. I'm just not going to make it for the inspection."

Without the inspection, the party couldn't happen at all.

Julie must have looked awful because Ivy and Myrtle—the new arrival—were hemming her in on either side. Ivy had a grip on her elbow like the claw of a lobster. Myrtle was rubbing Julie's back.

"What happened? Is it Ida?" The old woman sounded so worn, so fearful, that it snapped Julie out of her panic.

"No. No, Gram is fine. That was Ted, the inspector. He's… stuck in Boston. He can't do the inspection. We can't have the party." Julie raised her hand to her mouth and tried hard not to picture the disappointment on Gram's face when she came all this way for nothing. And Julie had worked so hard, too, to make this year extra special. "What am I going to do? I'll have to call Gram. Call the guests—"

"No," Myrtle snapped. "Don't. Don't do anything hasty."

"She's right," Ivy said. "Surely there's another way. Maybe you can get some kind of extension or variance due to extenuating circumstances. Or you could do the inspection via video call? This is the twenty-first century."

"Let me find out." Myrtle was already punching in numbers on her phone. She put the call on speakerphone and laid the cell on the counter as it rang.

Ted picked up on the second ring. "Hello?"

"Ted Thorndike, what on earth are you doing in

Boston?"

Ted gave a gusty sigh. "News travels fast, I see. Look, Myrtle, I'd be there if I could. There's just no way. I'd be risking my neck to drive in this."

"What about something else? A video inspection?"

He gave a chuckle that sounded entirely without humor. "I wish our policies were that up to date. No, it has to be in person. And I checked before I called. There's no one else who can do it. I'm so sorry."

"Why did you even drive all the way up to Boston knowing there was a storm on the way?"

"I didn't know! I swear it."

"All you had to do was turn to the weather channel."

He sighed. "I know, Myrtle. Believe me, I know. But I had some time off, and Klaus gave me these tickets to a Bruins game as a thank-you for some work I did for him earlier this year, and..."

"So, this is Klaus Miller's fault?"

Ted stammered on the other line, trying to correct her, but Myrtle mashed the button to end the call. She was fuming so visibly that smoke might as well have been billowing out from her ears. She snatched the phone away and put it in her pocket.

"I'll pick up the food later, Ivy. Julie, *don't do anything*. I'll fix this."

Baffled, Julie asked, "How?"

Myrtle's mouth tightened into a determined line. "I'm not sure, but I have an idea."

❄

"Is it even possible to throw the Christmas party without serving food?" Julie sighed as she piled groceries into the fridge. On another day, she would put more effort into it, making sure everything was in its proper place and easy to find. Today, she just shoved it in there and closed the door, leaning her weight against it.

Kringle patted at the bag of cat treats she'd placed on the countertop. He was clearly of the opinion that food was a necessity.

"Stop that. I'll give you one later. And you shouldn't even be up there."

Looking her in the eyes, he pushed the bag of treats off the counter. It thwacked onto the floor.

Julie rolled her eyes. "Classy." She retrieved the bag and returned it to the counter before unceremoniously dumping Kringle on the floor in place of the treats.

So, she couldn't throw the party without the catering. Gram would be heartbroken. No—Julie refused to wallow. She just didn't have the time.

Instead, she thumbed through the recent calls list on her phone. It was time to think out of the box.

The caterer picked up on the first ring. Before Jessica even finished with her greeting, Julie jumped in and said, "This is Julie from the Cozy Holly Inn. We can't get the inspection—Ted is indisposed. Is there any way we can find a workaround?"

"A workaround to the permit?" The woman on the other end of the line sounded skeptical. "The town is strict about these things. I'd be risking my business if I went ahead with the catering without your permit."

"But what if we can find another way?"

"I can't think of any. And what's wrong with Ted?"

Julie sighed. She tried to keep the frustration out of her voice as she answered, "He's stuck in Boston. What if you cooked the food and brought it? I know it might be cold but…"

"I can't."

Julie was starting to hate those two words.

Jessica continued, "I cook on site for a reason. It's why I was so excited about the two ovens you have at the inn. I just don't have the space at home. Maybe if you could find a place nearby?"

Julie gritted her teeth. "Yeah, right. The only place close by is Barrington Lodge. There's no way

Klaus would be willing to help us out." If she was reading between the lines right, he had deliberately planned to have the inspector stuck in Boston and unable to complete the inspection. No, Klaus and his too-small, Grinch of a heart were getting exactly what they wanted.

She was going to have to call off the party.

Head throbbing, she shut her eyes and tried to think. "Is there any other way you can think of?"

She didn't hear Jessica's answer because of the rumble of a car pulling up in front of the inn. That had to be Julie's parents with Gram. At least they'd been able to beat the storm by flying into New Hampshire instead of Boston. She'd run out of time to fix this before their arrival. And she felt even worse for having gotten this close to bringing Gram's dreams true only to have to dash them in the end.

"I have to go. Sorry—I'll call back."

Julie hung up the line and tried to pull herself together. She couldn't go out there on the verge of tears. She pinched the bridge of her nose. She was an adult. She could handle this. Somehow.

Don't do anything. Myrtle's words.

Julie looked at the cat, who was disdainfully cleaning himself on the kitchen floor. "All right, Myrtle. It's your play. You'd better bring us a miracle."

CHAPTER 31

*P*inecone Falls had really pulled through. Not that Nolan was surprised about it. He had only to drive into town and talk to one person about needing some last-minute decorations for the Lodge. Before he knew it, everyone in town was coming up to him and slipping something out of their pocket or purse. An ornament for the tree. A snow globe. Ivy even threw in an edible dog treat tree ornament.

That probably wouldn't last long on the tree once Snowball noticed it.

By the time he'd returned to the house, Gramps and his dad had cut down the biggest tree Nolan had ever seen. It was a shame the thing would have to wait until tomorrow to be decorated because he had shopping bags full of ornaments for it. Not to mention the strings of lights, garlands, and other things he had picked up from a local store.

Upon seeing him step through the front door of Barrington House, Stan laughed. "What, did you buy out the whole town?"

Nolan set down the bags next to the huge tree in the corner. A double stairway curled up to either side of the front desk, leading to the wing of guest rooms. None of it had been decorated yet, but Stan and Gramps were bent over the tidy box of his mother's old Christmas decorations, sorting through the items left.

Shaking his head in chagrin, Nolan said, "This is only the first batch. I have more in the truck. Word gets around fast, and the whole town came out to add to the takings. Gramps, I have your old tree topper in here. Barney from town kept it rather than selling it in his antique shop."

The look on Gramps's face was priceless. Nolan bent to riffle through the bags until he found the star tree topper Gramps loved so much. He smiled as he reached out gnarled hands to take it.

"I had this one since I was a boy. Never should have thrown it out."

Gramps looked so frail that Nolan wanted to hug him. But he knew how unwanted such displays of emotion were, so he turned on his heel and marched out through the door for the second load.

It was the mark of a canine nose that Snowball was somehow able to smell the ornamental dog treat before Nolan fully walked through the door. His dog dashed out of the interior of the house, her tail churning the air, to stick her nose inside the bag holding it. Nolan laughed. "Not now, Snowball. You'll get it on Christmas."

Stan watched the dog with an uncharacteristically fond smile. "Do you remember your old dog, Rudolph?"

He and Gramps were rummaging through the bags already deposited in the entryway and pulling out the ornaments fit to decorate the main rooms of Barrington Lodge. Gramps had fistfuls of the faux-pine garland that seemed to go on forever. Nolan had picked up some real pine boughs to mix in with them that would add a nice scent to the rooms.

Nolan smiled, reaching down to pet his dog. "How could I forget? You and Mom gave him to me on Christmas when I was five."

"You wanted a dog," Stan said with a laugh. He helped Gramps extricate the rest of the garland, and without talking about it out loud, they both moved toward the left-hand staircase to wrap it around the railing.

"I'm not sure Rudolph counted as a dog. More like a small horse."

Stan laughed again. "That dog sure could run."

"Yeah, at the most inopportune times." Nolan pulled out the one delicate item from the bags that seemed most vulnerable to Snowball, the ornamental dog treat. He hung it out of reach on the otherwise-empty tree, much to the dog's dismay. She whined and pawed at his leg, but he held firm. She was a well-pampered dog. She would survive a couple days of drooling at that treat.

After toeing off his snow-crusted winter boots, Nolan lengthened his stride to help his family with the garland. "Do you remember that time Rudolph took off with the Christmas lights?"

"Do I?" His dad groaned. "They were still attached to the house! That dog pulled the brackets right off the eaves, and I had to climb up and drill new holes."

"I remember Rudolph," Gramps said slowly as if he might be mixing up memories. "Poor thing never grew into his nose."

"That's the dog," Nolan said with a laugh. "Mom used to put reindeer ears on the poor thing every Christmas for the family Christmas card contest."

"Did I ever tell you how she started that?" Stan asked.

"*Mom* started that awful tradition? I *hated* sitting for those photos. It felt like she was trying to dress me up in something Christmassy for every Halloween, just to get those pictures in time!"

Stan gave a full belly laugh and leaned against the railing. "Your aunt Agatha was worse. She'd start in September!"

"I guess I should feel lucky not to be my cousins, but still… the photos couldn't wait until the snow came at least?"

"Your grandmother loved those cards," Gramps said fondly. It had been a long time since his wife had passed, long enough that Nolan couldn't really remember her.

"Did she?"

"Oh, yes. Especially the ones from when you were a baby. Do you still have those ones, Stan? She and Agatha seemed to be competing for most elaborate baby costume every year."

"Nolan always cried," Stan said with a smile. He looked up and rubbed the back of his neck, gauging the distance to the top of the banister. They were only halfway done and almost out of garland. They were going to need two per staircase.

Luckily, Nolan had gone overboard when buying the decorations for a reason. Barrington Lodge was a big place.

287

"Of course I cried," Nolan complained, not that he could remember the photo shoots from when he was a baby. He'd seen the aftermath, though. Baby Santa, complete with beard. A little elf with rosy cheeks. An angel with fluffy wings. Or the most terrible of them all... "The gingerbread was the worst. I looked more like Raggedy Andy."

"The gingerbread!" Stan exclaimed. "That was the best one. You matched us, son. If I had to wear that costume, you should count yourself lucky you only had to wear it once. Okay, twice. Maybe three times."

Gramps said, "I think he came to Christmas dinner dressed like a gingerbread."

"Believe it or not, that was actually your favorite one. You refused to take it off."

"I was two. I refuse to take responsibility for my decisions at that age."

Gramps laughed, a long chuckle Nolan hadn't heard in far too long. It was nice, having them to talk with again, to share memories. Maybe even to make more. But the stories all revolved around Nolan's mom, a force of nature. What would it be like to have a force of nature like that in his life, pushing him into holiday cheer?

Or would he be the one to take after his mom? It was a nice thought. A warm thought. And when he thought of the future, he couldn't help but think of Julie. He wanted someone to share the holidays with, to make new memories, new traditions.

And yes, maybe even to compete in the crazy family Christmas card contest. He had the sense that Julie was the kind of woman who would jump right into it with him.

His warm thoughts were cut off by the slam of the front door as it opened. Nolan lost his end of the garland, and it started to unravel until caught by Stan. In the middle of the doorway was a tiny woman, and she did not look happy.

"Klaus Miller, what did you do?" Myrtle demanded.

Gramps blinked, taken aback. He looked at the tree, the garland, and then at her again. "What do you mean? I've been here all day."

Scowling, Myrtle shut the front door with just as much force as she'd opened it. Snowball plastered her ears to her head and shrank away from the sound.

Without taking off her snowy boots, Myrtle marched off the welcome mat and onto the clean hardwood floors. Her boots squeaked. At the bottom of the stairs, she pressed her hands to her hips and glared up at them. Nolan battled the urge to slip away. For a small woman, she could look fearsome.

"You know what I mean. You sent Ted Thorndike

to Boston *knowing* he would get caught in the storm and be unable to complete the inspection. You sabotaged Ida's party!"

Nolan tied off the end of his garland so it wouldn't slip. "The party is off? But…" Julie had been working so hard. She would be devastated. "Is there anything I can do?"

He started down the stairs, only to find his way blocked by Klaus's outstretched arm.

"Not you. You didn't cause this trouble."

Disappointment settled over Nolan. He'd thought his grandfather and father had turned a corner. They'd been so cheery, and here they were decorating, but if what Myrtle said was true… this vendetta against the Greens was going too far. "Gramps…"

His grandfather ignored the warning in his tone, turning instead to look down the stairs at Myrtle. "I didn't know about the storm. Maybe I thought buying some goodwill with Ted would make him remember well of me, but… I didn't outright plan for him not to show up to the inspection."

Myrtle didn't look convinced. She looked more likely to storm up the stairs and wag her finger in Gramps's face. When the old man raised his hands in surrender, Nolan could have pushed past him. He didn't. That had sounded like genuine regret in Gramps's voice. Had his outlook changed?

"It's the truth, Myrtle. I'm… turning over a new leaf." He gestured to Stan. "We both are. I was just returning a favor that I owed to Ted. I had no idea he would end up stranded in Boston or that would somehow ruin the Cozy Holly Inn party. How do we fix this?"

Myrtle scoffed. "This isn't the first time you've been a grouch to Ida Green. You want me to believe you're suddenly Mr. Nice Guy?"

Gramps moved with difficulty as he descended the stairs. He clung to the railing to steady himself, his fingers brushing the false greenery. "I know how I've been. But I do want to help."

"Right." Myrtle crossed her arms. "And what brought on this change of opinion?"

Gramps glanced up the stairs to Nolan. Was he looking for help answering that question? Nolan didn't have the first idea what had led to this change of heart. He didn't want to look at it too closely. All he wanted was to encourage this new, softened version of his grandfather.

Myrtle said, "I see. Well. What problem have you even had with Ida all these years? She's got a good heart, and you know she doesn't go about stealing your customers, especially not now."

Gramps cleared his throat. His shoulders bowed in a way that looked almost sheepish. "She never invited me to her fancy Christmas parties. Not once."

Nolan couldn't believe his ears. "*That's* what this is about?" He walked down the steps to stand abreast of Gramps, but the old man didn't look him in the eye.

Nor did he justify the answer. It was the only answer they were likely to get.

Myrtle narrowed her eyes. Her mouth had a pinched quality as she thought. "Are your permits current?"

"Of course." Gramps sounded offended at the question.

Myrtle pulled out her phone. "Then let me see if we can fix this. It must be young Jessica who's doing the catering now." Myrtle scrolled through her contact list for so long that Nolan wondered whether she had the phone numbers of everyone in town on there. He wouldn't be surprised. "Ah." She dialed then held the phone to her ear.

Everyone collectively held their breaths.

"Jessica, dear? It's Myrtle. Yes, from the shelter. How is Fluffy? Good to hear. Listen, I have a question for you about the party at the Cozy Holly Inn." She paused, squinting as she listened, and nodded along to the other end of the conversation. "Yes, I know you need the permit in order to do the cooking. That's why I'm calling. Would the kitchens at Barrington Lodge work? They're bigger and—yes. Yes, of course. I'll figure that part out. You just worry about making the food. Thanks, bye."

Satisfied, the old woman punched the button to end the call and slid the phone into her pocket. Each one of the Miller men had his eyes on her, waiting for her to explain the call.

In a no-nonsense tone, she told Gramps, "She'll be doing the cooking for the party in your kitchen. All we have to do is figure out how to get it up to the Cozy Holly Inn while it's still hot. If we cut through the woods, it's not far, though that's going to be a bit of a struggle in the snow."

Nolan suggested, "Why not take the sleigh? We were going to dust it off anyway for the season. After the food has been delivered, we could offer sleigh rides."

"I like that plan," Stan said as he joined them at the bottom of the stairs. "The trip will be a little narrow in parts, but it should be no trouble for a skilled driver like me."

That answered who was going to shuttle the food back and forth.

Only Gramps looked unconvinced. "I just don't see how Ida will agree to it. That woman is as stubborn as molasses. She doesn't like accepting help from anybody."

Nolan pointed out, "She's had Julie planning this entire thing. She obviously doesn't mind anymore."

"That's different. Julie's her granddaughter."

With a cat-got-the-cream smile, Myrtle said, "Leave that part to me."

CHAPTER 32

*G*ram was enchanted. There was no other word for the look on her face as she'd toured the first floor of the inn. Now, sitting in her customary chair by the Christmas tree with Kringle on her lap and a cup of hot chocolate in her hands, Gram looked like she was living out a dream. Every time she'd given Julie a bit of praise, Julie had simultaneously soaked up the warmth of her gram's approval and inwardly cringed. She hadn't mentioned the lack of a permit and the trouble with the caterer yet. She was still hoping that Myrtle would bring a miracle. But the longer she and her family sat curled up in the living room reminiscing, the more she realized that this was one thing none of them could fix. And she had come so close!

With idle strokes, Gram petted Kringle's soft fur.

The cat had decided to act charming today, and raised his head for her ministrations, purring all the while. Julie tried not to be too bitter about it. After all, he had thawed considerably toward her too.

Gram exclaimed, "Do you remember that one year Julie decided to be the tree?"

"I what?" Julie asked with a laugh.

Next to her on the sofa, her mother chuckled. "You always had to be underfoot when Gram was decorating the tree."

Gram said, "I think you were two or three. You wrapped yourself in one of the garlands and informed us all that you were the tree that year and we had to decorate you."

"I don't remember this at all! Dad?"

"I remember," her dad said. He was dressed as she always remembered him, in one of his black polo shirts and a pair of slacks. For Christmas he would wear some color, at Mom's insistence, but only then. "We had to decorate you with candy canes."

Mom said, "Trying to take them away from you afterward was the real trial. I'm sure you were still holding on to two when you fell asleep that night."

Contrary to Dad's solemn fashion choice, Mom always seemed to have walked straight out of a runway. Her blouse was splashed with color like an abstract painting, and her patterned leggings drew the eye down to her bare feet, where she'd painted her toes red. She had a rich, full laugh that Julie had always loved and that warmed her even now when she was soon to be the bearer of bad news.

Not yet. She'd find the right moment, just… not when they were in the middle of happy memories.

Gram, her cozy Christmas sweater gaining a coating of white fur that she didn't seem to notice, said, "You had your first kiss here too. When you were four or five, I think."

Julie covered her face with her hands. "Oh my gosh. Please tell me it wasn't with Nolan Miller."

"I really can't recall," Gram said in a tone of voice that bespoke otherwise. "But I do remember your gramps took aside the young man in question and told him in no uncertain terms that he'd best marry you when you grew up."

"That is beyond embarrassing." Julie's cheeks felt hot beneath the shield of her hands. At least there was one thing to be thankful for—if it *had* been Nolan, he didn't remember the incident any more than she did.

When she looked up from between her fingers, Gram was looking at her with a twinkle in her eye. "Why are you so worried it would be with Nolan, dear?"

Julie did *not* want to answer that question. Instead,

she changed the subject. "You look good, Gram. The drive doesn't seem to have tired you out any."

"Oh, I'm sure these old bones won't thank me for it in the morning. I'm not meant for traveling around anymore.

She studied Gram. Her cheeks were rosy, and she was smiling. No hint of a cough or even a wheeze. She'd sounded so awful on the phone before. Had it really just been nothing? "You sound well, Gram. Glad your cough is gone."

Gram waved her hand dismissively. "A minor cough. I'm fit as a fiddle. In fact, I'd stay here and run the inn myself if I had someone young and strong to help."

Julie forgot how to breathe. Slowly, she lowered her hands to her lap. It was what she had been thinking herself, only a few days ago, wasn't it? And a nice dream it was, to think of waking up at the inn every morning to birds chirping rather than to the irritable sounds of traffic. To stop in at the grocery store, where the cashier knew you by name and asked after your family, instead of hastily putting your order through and clocking out for a break.

But that's just what it was—a dream. Julie didn't want to shatter it, but the responsibilities of her real life had already started creeping in. "I have a job interview in Boston on the twenty-seventh."

"A job interview?" Mom exclaimed. "That's wonderful. Where is it?"

At the same time, Dad muttered, "Two days after Christmas? That's outrageous!"

Julie chose to answer her mom. "It's at a big magazine company. The same one where my friend Cheryl works. It would be a permanent position on the writing team."

"Congratulations!" Mom wrapped an arm around her.

Julie tried not to make a face as her mom squeezed the air out of her. "I haven't gotten the job yet. Only an interview."

"I know you will nail that interview. You're an incredible writer, and they'd be lucky to have you."

Julie didn't know whether her mom actually read most of the articles she wrote, but she knew that Mom, like Gram, collected them and the magazines they were published in.

Gram said, "We're proud of you, but I thought we'd have more time together this year to celebrate."

So had Julie. Three days were just not enough, especially if Myrtle worked a miracle, and they were putting on that party tomorrow. Softly, she said, "I know… but this is a really good move for my career."

But now that she thought about it, was it really a dream career, or just a job? She'd thrown herself into becoming a writer, determined to make it. Maybe working for magazine after magazine in which she was assigned projects rather than choosing what she would write about wasn't what she had initially thought she would be doing, but there were a lot of writers who didn't get to write for a living at all. She was one of the lucky few. The successful few. Wasn't she?

She really wanted to write what she wanted to write, maybe freelance articles she could sell or even a book. But that sort of work wasn't stable. It didn't pay the bills. But if she had another job that left her plenty of time to write…

Gram interrupted her thoughts. "We'll be together at Christmas this year; that's all that matters. And you've done such a wonderful job preparing the inn for the Christmas party!"

This was it, the perfect opening for her to tell them the truth. That the party probably wasn't going to happen. She dropped her gaze to her knees and muttered, "About that…"

"What is it?" Mom asked.

"There's a problem. With the party. We need a special permit for the caterer to use our kitchen, and she can't cook at home and bring the food. I already asked. The inspector is stuck in Boston. We can't get the permit. Gram, I'm so sorry…"

Julie felt like crying. Again, her mom squeezed her shoulders, but this time it was a gentler hug.

"We'll figure it out," Gram said with conviction. "We can't let all this hard work go to waste. If we need to, we'll do all the cooking ourselves!"

Someone knocked on the door. Yawning, Kringle stretched and jumped off Gram's lap, trotting toward the door as if he could open it and let the person in.

The knock came again, more vigorously this time.

Julie got to her feet at the same time as Gram did. Despite the way she'd sounded on the phone a few days ago, Gram was as robust as ever. She reached the door before Julie made it into the hallway.

"Ida, open up!" came the muffled voice from the other side.

Gram opened the door as Myrtle had her fist raised to knock again. Her face was flushed, her hat on askew.

"Myrtle, it's so good to see you!"

Myrtle accepted a hug but made it brief. "No time for this now. Put your boots on and come out back. I have a solution to your catering problem."

She must have worked a miracle, after all.

Julie and her parents, who had clustered behind her in the doorway to the hall, rushed to grab boots and coats and follow the two women into the cold outdoors. Myrtle made a motion for Julie and her parents to stay back, but when Julie saw the string of footsteps in the snow leading not to Myrtle's car but to the tree line leading toward Barrington Lodge, she rushed around the porch to catch a closer glimpse.

Klaus stood alone at the edge of the trees, shoulders bowed, and hands stuffed into the pockets of his winter coat. Behind him, far enough away to give him privacy, stood Stan and Nolan. As she watched, Gram and Myrtle made their way toward Klaus. Myrtle stopped well back to give the pair privacy, but nearer to the inn than the others on Klaus's side.

"What do you think they're saying?" Mom asked as she joined Julie at the rail. She rubbed her hands together and blew on them.

"I have no idea," Julie muttered. When she looked past the speaking pair to Nolan again, she found him watching her. He nodded, his smile visible even at this distance. She couldn't help but smile back. She raised her hand in a wave.

No, she didn't know what Gram and Klaus were talking about, but suddenly she had the hope that maybe, this was all going to work out fine.

She and her parents huddled by the porch rail until Gram shook hands with Klaus, turned, and made leisurely progress back toward the inn with Myrtle, the two of them laughing and smiling. The moment she came within earshot, Julie couldn't contain herself any longer.

"Well?" she asked.

Gram cracked a smile. "We're using the lodge kitchens for the party."

Mom, who seemed a bit more suspicious than Gram, asked, "That's it? The party is on, just like that?"

"Well," Gram said, "we are going to have a few additional guests."

Julie looked up again at the tree line, but the Millers were gone. "Guests?" she asked, hoping. She had already unofficially invited Nolan, but she hadn't broached the subject with Gram.

"Klaus, Stan, and Nolan will be coming, too, along with all the people currently booked at Barrington Lodge."

Myrtle really had managed to pull off a miracle. And it was a good thing Julie had made extra party favors, just in case a particularly ornery cat broke one. This was going to be a Christmas party to remember.

CHAPTER 33

The late-afternoon sunlight cast Julie's room in shades of orange and gold. Downstairs in the kitchen, the serving staff were arranging things to their liking, including the enormous bowl of punch Julie and Gram had mixed up earlier that day and left to chill in the fridge. She and Gram had also worked in tandem to give the inn a quick cleaning and lay out the small white boxes containing this year's party favors. Gram had been delighted with the work Julie had put into them, and Julie had retreated upstairs to get ready for the party with a smile wide enough that her cheeks ached.

Up until she entered her room, a towel wrapped around her wet hair, to discover the mess her dress had become. "Kringle!"

The cat, curled up on the red fabric and donating

what looked to be half of his fur, blinked slowly at her. That blink said plainly, *If you didn't want me to sit on it, you shouldn't have left it out.*

Julie sighed. She shooed him off the dress and vigorously brushed it off. One thing she stupidly hadn't thought to buy was a lint brush. In her defense, she hadn't lived with a cat for years, let alone a long-haired cat like Kringle. When she finally decided that the dress was as clean as it was going to get, she slid into it.

Her phone rang.

Julie hopped on one foot and nearly crashed to the floor. She rarely got cell signal in her room. Her phone was plugged into the charger at the moment, in the furthest corner of the room. Stooping so she didn't have to unplug it, with one leg in the dress and the other still out of it, Julie answered the call.

"Hello?"

"Congratulations on the interview! Why didn't you tell me when you got the call?"

Cheryl's voice crackled across the line, almost unfamiliar. Julie felt guilty. She'd been so busy with the party plans and the wrenches thrown into them that she hadn't even thought of her life in Boston. But she couldn't tell that to Cheryl. Cheryl had been a good friend, getting her résumé in front of the right people for Julie to get that call to begin with.

"Sorry. I didn't think it was a big deal. I was going to tell you after if I got the job."

"Not a big deal!" Cheryl exclaimed. "Of course it's a big deal! You're one of only three applicants they're interviewing. You've got a real shot at getting this job, Julie. What outfit are you planning on wearing? It's a fashion mag, you have to look your best."

Julie, who had glanced down at the red dress before realizing that her friend was still chattering about the interview, said, "I hadn't thought that far ahead. Most of my wardrobe is still in Boston."

It was an excuse, and Cheryl heard it as one. "You're going to have to do better than that. Are you going to get your hair done before the interview?"

"The day after Christmas?" Julie hadn't planned on it. She hadn't planned on anything, in fact. Even thinking about it now, she couldn't dredge up a spark of excitement. She was too nervous about tonight's party going off without a hitch.

"I'm sure there's a salon open somewhere up there in the middle of nowhere."

Julie made a noncommittal sound. Her hair looked fine as it was.

"I bet you can't wait to get out of Podunk, Vermont, and back to your regular life. I can't believe you lasted this long! I honestly thought you'd be back in Boston commiserating with me over drinks."

"I know, right?" Julie had thought so too… at first. But now, she wasn't sure she would be happy to leave Pinecone Falls behind. Her life had taken a complete one-eighty from where it had been before she'd driven out here. She hadn't thought she'd like the quiet, small-town life, but now she had friends here. She had a purpose and a reason to keep busy rather than spending all her free time scrolling through social media. She hadn't even thought about the city or Instagram in days.

"What?" Cheryl asked. "You're breaking up."

In the background, Julie heard sleigh bells. Raising her voice, she told her friend, "I have to go. Sorry! Talk to you later." She hung up without even waiting for Cheryl's response and quickly shimmied the rest of the way into the red dress.

When she hurried to the window, she caught sight of the horse-drawn sleigh coming through the woods. Stan sat up front, guiding the brown-and-white horses through the tricky, winding path. Nolan sat next to him, with Klaus, the caterer, and the first batch of food in the sleigh itself.

Julie grinned. She hurried to shake out her hair and brush it, the last thing she needed to do since she'd already applied her makeup in the bathroom. Her hair was still damp, but rather than taking the time to blow-dry it, she hurried downstairs to help with the food. The party was about to begin.

❄

IT HAD BEEN A FEW YEARS SINCE NOLAN HAD HITCHED one of their horses to the sleigh but driving it had come back as if it had been yesterday. The bay gelding stamped his feet and whipped his tail through the air to show his irritation at keeping still after they stopped behind the Cozy Holly Inn. Nolan moved to his head and rubbed the blaze down the center of the horse's forehead. "You and me both, buddy," he muttered under his breath.

Today was the probably last day he would see Julie—unless he did something drastic. Something like ask her to stay. He'd tried keeping his distance, but that hadn't helped. He *liked* her. He wanted to get to know her better. He wanted to hold her in his arms again. But he couldn't do that if she fled to her old life in Boston. But what was he asking her to consider, by staying? His family was buying the Cozy Holly Inn. There was nothing here for her.

Maybe he could convince her to stay for the transition, make sure the inn was in good hands or something to that effect. Maybe his efforts were doomed from the start. But if he said nothing, she would definitely leave.

He had to take a chance.

The horses snorted steam into the air. Nolan murmured sweet nonsense while he stroked their noses. His dad and Gramps had already gotten out of the sleigh and were cheerfully joking with the caterer as they helped bring the steam-filled containers inside the inn's kitchen through the back door.

"Nolan," Gramps snapped. "Quit your daydreaming and come to help."

Nolan gave the horses' necks a pat and accepted a round container from Gramps. Dutifully, he brought it inside, where several others had already been laid out along the kitchen counter. The serving staff—two teenagers in black pants, white shirts, and aprons—were busy arranging the appetizers onto trays to bring into the party. Nolan found an empty space along the counter to leave his burden and started to back out to get another. There was a lot of food.

"Is that little Nolan Miller?"

Nolan didn't recognize the man's voice, but his face—dirty-blond hair threaded with gray and eyes the same shape and color as Julie's—gave away the relation to Julie. Nolan, who was taller than the older man by a good half a foot, automatically reached out to grip the offered hand.

"Not so little anymore, sir."

Julie's dad laughed. "No need to be so formal. Call me Greg."

The woman by his side wearing the velvet green dress must be Julie's mother, then. She turned, and he recognized her from his childhood days.

"Nolan Miller!" She pulled him into a hug before he knew what was happening.

"Nice to see you, Mrs. Green."

An old woman he did immediately recognize shouldered her way through the kitchen.

"If you people have time to chat, you have time to help the catering staff arrange plates." Ida Green, a force to be reckoned with even at her age, swatted her son and daughter-in-law away. Nolan was glad for the breathing room. When she held out her arms, he gave her a quick hug. She came up to the middle of his chest.

"Thank you for your help. If all the food is inside, why don't you take off your coat and grab yourself a cup of punch? Julie should be down any minute."

Nolan lost whatever he'd been about to say when the woman in question strode into the room. She wore a red dress that hugged her curves and ended just above the knee. Her hair was loose, still clinging to her face in damp waves. Nolan raised his hand and caught her eye. When she smiled, he forgot to breathe. She was gorgeous.

Meanwhile, he still wore his barn jacket with the nearest hat shoved onto his head for the drive. He pulled the hat from his head and ran his fingers through his hair, hoping that he didn't look too unkempt in comparison. He met her just inside the doorway and touched her lightly on the elbow.

"I was hoping we'd have a chance to talk before the party got into full swing."

When Julie took his hand, he closed his fingers around hers on instinct. Her hand was so small, her fingers so elegant compared to his. They fit together. She glanced around the chaos of the kitchen—his dad and grandfather were entering with the last of the food—and tugged Nolan into the hall. Even in here, there were little decorations that reminded him of her. Snowflakes strung along the top of the wall. Wrapping paper carefully tucked and taped around the light switch. He smiled and tightened his grip on her hand. When Julie did something, she went all in. He admired that about her.

In the cooler air of the hall—the heat of so many bodies packed into such a closed space was suffocating, to say the least—Julie let out a breath. She blew an errant strand of her hair out of her eyes.

"I had no idea throwing one Christmas party was

so much work! I thought I'd already taken care of everything, but Gram has had me running around in circles all day. And a friend just reminded me about my interview in two days. Two days! I can't believe it's snuck up on me so fast. I can't even think about anything else now." She sighed, then squeezed his hand and looked up at him. "Sorry. I'm glad you're here. Thank you for all the help you and your family are doing to pull this off. We honestly couldn't put on this party without you."

"It's no trouble," he said truthfully. He wanted to pull Julie into his arms and hug her, center her, but that wasn't his role here. He untangled their fingers and pulled away.

She didn't seem to notice but combed her fingers through her hair. "What did you want to talk about?"

Stay in Pinecone Falls. Right. The chances she would do that after she'd just heaped all her excitement about the interview onto him were less than nil. He shoved his hands into his pockets, balling one around the cold wool of his hat. "Nothing important. You look nice today."

He had the satisfaction of watching her cheeks turn pink. She felt something for him, but... it probably wasn't enough.

You won't know unless you ask.

"Thank you. You look nice too."

He laughed. "You're assuming I do. I haven't even taken off my coat yet."

Her blush deepened. "You always do."

Her words were overshadowed by her grandmother's sharp call. "Julie! Come in here and help with the appetizers. The guests will be arriving soon!"

She glanced into the kitchen before meeting Nolan's gaze again. "Are you sure it was nothing?"

Ask.

He took a step away from her instead. "I'm sure," he said. He let her walk away, chiding himself for watching as she left. And for wishing they had longer to talk, to get to know each other.

There was no point in getting to know a woman who was hours away from walking out of his life.

CHAPTER 34

*J*ulie wished she had more time with Nolan. When she'd pictured putting on the party, this was the part of the evening when she'd envisioned she'd get to sit back and enjoy herself. It was Christmas Eve! Instead, Gram had her arranging crab puffs on a plate.

The doorbell rang.

"Julie," Gram called.

Julie hurried to finish off the tray and called back, "I've got it." She wiped her fingers on a kitchen towel with embroidered mistletoe in the corners.

By the time she reached the front door, Gram was on her heels. She opened the door and smiled at the first arrivals. To her surprise, it didn't feel forced. By now, Julie had spoken with over half the town with her stops in for groceries or to meet with Ivy. They weren't strangers. The first three arrivals, in fact, were friends. Myrtle had barely taken off her coat, which Julie hung over her arm to transfer to one of the beds upstairs, when Ivy and her husband pulled up to the inn.

She hugged both of them tight. "Thank you so much for coming."

"Thank you for inviting me," Ivy said with a wink. "I figured I'd be left out because I'm too young for the traditional crowd."

"That may be changing," Gram said warmly. "Julie needs some friends her own age here too. Why don't you all go into the living room? Nolan and Klaus Miller are already in there by the fire."

Julie wanted to join them, but another vehicle pulled into the large area beside the circular driveway, which had been plowed earlier in the day to accommodate parking. Then another. All were faces Julie recognized. Lucy and her mother from the café. Al Henderson, the owner of the grocery store in town. When Ned Wheatley arrived and Julie's arms were overflowing with coats, she told him, "Wait right here. I have something for you."

She disappeared upstairs, and on the way back, picked up the picture she had found of Ned and his brother. The old man was making himself comfortable in the dining room, which was filling with an increasing number of people, when she found him again. When she presented him with the picture, his eyes watered.

"That's me and my brother."

"I know." She could have walked away under the pretense of greeting more of the guests—there were faces here now she didn't even recognize, one of them being the middle-aged woman who had been chatting with Ned when she'd walked up. Instead, she leaned over his shoulder and looked at the picture with him. "Which one is you? You two look so alike, I can't tell."

With a watery chuckle, Ned pointed out the man on the left. He then launched into a charming story about a prank he and his brother had once played on Gram during one of these parties. Julie found herself laughing and relaxing. She liked chatting with him, even though they didn't know each other well. And when he reached out to squeeze her hand with a thank-you, her chest warmed.

It was surprisingly nice to find herself in this position, able to talk to people in the role of hostess. A heck of a lot better than being stuffed into a cubicle and asked to churn out an increasing number of daily words, like she was a lemon squeezed for the last bit of juice.

She turned to the woman, who Gram must have

greeted in her stead. "I'm sorry, but I don't remember you."

The woman chuckled. "You wouldn't. I'm staying at Barrington Lodge over Christmas. You are so lucky to live in this beautiful town."

I would be lucky, Julie thought. She didn't live here, and in fact, would have to leave tomorrow night if she wanted to be back in Boston in time to prepare for her interview. It felt like another world, another life.

When she left the pair, she found that the house had filled up with guests. The parking area was full, and the driveway was lined on one side with cars, leaving just enough space for a vehicle to squeeze past on the way out. Not that anyone seemed inclined to leave. Julie paused in the arch to the living room. Lights sparkled from the windows and the Christmas tree. The air smelled of pine and the freshly baked appetizers circulating the room. Around her, guests laughed and chattered, one voice blending into the next. The party was a success. She grinned.

She spotted Myrtle posing by the tree while Gram took her photo using a digital camera. Julie navigated the room until she could take the camera from Gram. Along the way, she caught snatches of conversation, stories being told of past parties and how this one compared. In her eyes, this one was the best of all.

Then again, she had been a kid or a teenager for the others. Not exactly interested in spending time with people her mom or Gram's age.

"Let me take one." Julie had to shout to be heard over the rest of the partygoers. She took the camera from Gram and ushered her into place next to Myrtle. Julie snapped more than one photo, just in case the first one turned out badly. The moment she started to put down the camera and Myrtle stepped away, someone else claimed the spot next to Gram. Julie took another photo, and another, and another until Myrtle tugged the camera out of her hand.

"Let me. If this is going to be the last party, we might as well make as many memories as we can."

She sounded sad. Despite the cheer of the party, Julie felt it too. It wasn't just that this would be the last Christmas Eve party thrown by the Cozy Holly Inn. This was the end of the Cozy Holly Inn. Soon it would become a part of Barrington Lodge.

What had Gram said about staying? But that was a dream, a what-if. The reality was that this house all but belonged to someone else now.

Julie forced her shoulders back and faked a cheerful smile until it became natural. It was easy. Every knot of guests she stopped at to say hello had stories to tell of the past, of how much the inn meant to them. It was more than a business, more than a place to stay while someone was here on vacation. It was a part of the community. And so was Gram, even if she'd been away for the last long while.

Her stomach grumbling, Julie managed to detach herself and pluck a glass of water from a server's tray and a couple appetizers on a napkin from another. She found the quietest corner of the dining room and wedged herself into it, watching the revelry from a distance. It was nice to talk to so many people who had fond memories of her family and her gram, but she needed a minute of breathing room.

Nolan found her there when she'd polished off the appetizers and had finished half the water. Without saying a word, he slid into place beside her, his back to the wall, and looked out to the gathering.

"I thought you might have left," she confessed.

"A party like this? Not a chance. You're a success." He toasted her with a glass of his own, this one filled with punch.

Julie felt her cheeks heat. "It's all Gram and the caterer. I just did the decorating."

"You did the lion's share of the work. Don't diminish yourself." He gave her a smile she felt down to her toes. "I'm glad it worked out in the end."

The relief Julie felt at the reminder of how this all might have been canceled was palpable. "That was a Christmas miracle, for sure. But why all the secrecy while Gram and your grandfather were talking? What do you think they were saying?"

"Who knows? He wouldn't tell me. But I know he felt a bit slighted that he'd never been invited to one of these parties."

Julie groaned. "Then why not just say something? I'm sure Gram just thought he would be too stubborn to attend the party of a business rival. She's never had a vendetta against him or anything, not that I know."

Nolan raised his eyebrows. "I think they're both too stubborn for their own good. Proud too."

Julie smirked. "You may be right about that."

Shifting position, Nolan turned his back on the gathering. With his attention fully on her, Julie felt a little self-conscious. She tucked a strand of hair behind her ear.

"But you know what really made the difference? *You.*"

Julie opened her mouth to protest that she hadn't done anything.

Nolan held up a hand. "You," he repeated. "And that picture you gave me. It really helped my dad to open up and let go of all that misery he's been holding in. Gramps too." Nolan swept a hand to a knot of people in the corner of the room. Stan was red-faced with laughter, and maybe from the punch too. "I haven't seen him laugh like that in years. Maybe since before Mom's diagnosis. And it never would have happened without you."

Again, he turned back to her, making her feel like the only person in the room. He caught her free hand, twining their fingers together. Could he feel the flutter of her pulse against his wrist? He studied her face, and although she wasn't certain what he was hoping to find in her expression, she couldn't look away.

So softly she wondered whether she might have misheard, he whispered, "Speaking of Christmas miracles… I wish you weren't leaving tomorrow."

Julie parted her lips but couldn't find her voice. He looked so earnest, so intense that it made her shiver. Was this the punch talking? Or was he asking her to stay in Pinecone Falls… for him?

"There you two are!"

Julie jumped at Gram's loud exclamation. She pulled her hand free of Nolan's, though her fingers still tingled. Her face probably matched her dress for color right now.

Gram was beaming. She stopped squarely in between them, putting her hands on the hips of a dress that, quite frankly, made her look a little like a thin Mrs. Claus. Her cheeks were a bit pink, too, likely because she had been no stranger to the Christmas punch.

She grabbed them both by an arm and squeezed. Hard. "I knew you two would get along as adults. Do you remember how you used to fight as kids?"

Julie risked a sidelong glance at Nolan, only to find him looking at her. A bit sheepish, he said, "I did find her a bit annoying."

Julie gaped. "*You* found *me* annoying?" That was like the pot calling the kettle black.

He laughed and raised his hands. "Not anymore. I think we've both grown out of that stage."

She smiled. "You could say that."

Myrtle joined them with cheeks just as jolly pink as Gram's and a smile just as wide. She linked her arm through Gram's and said in an overly loud voice, "Julie, I must congratulate you. You've put on the best Christmas party that I can remember."

Julie bit her lip and risked a glance at Gram. "I'm sure it's not the best one…"

Gram winked. "Take credit where credit is due. You did a fantastic job this year."

Julie hadn't had a sip of the punch yet, but her veins buzzed as if she had. She grinned.

Leaning closer to Gram but not doing much to lower her voice, Myrtle said, "I wish you would reconsider selling. This place still has a lot of life left in it."

Julie grimaced. Nolan's dad, and probably his grandfather, too, were just across the room. At that volume, the whole house probably heard.

Gram didn't look worried. Instead, she looked a little sad. She wrapped an arm around her friend's shoulders and squeezed. "I would. You know I would, Myrtle. But with no one to help run the inn, it's just not possible."

It's just not possible. That was what Julie had been telling herself the entire time. It was what she had told Kringle every time he rubbed against her palm and purred. What she told Ivy when they met for lunch at the café. What she would have had to tell Nolan if Gram hadn't interrupted their moment. Her life… it wasn't here.

At least, it hadn't been before ten days ago. But everyone around her, laughing, drinking too much punch, and singing Christmas carols off tune—they had each become a part of her. She'd started to build extra time into the errands she ran in town just so she could stop and chat about her family and the party. She loved waking up to birdsong instead of traffic horns. The Cozy Holly Inn was a piece of her childhood, home in a way that no other place had ever been.

Myrtle said, "What about Julie? She's done such a good job. I'd say that's a killer job interview."

Pressing her lips together, Gram shook her head. "Julie has a great opportunity in Boston. I'm so proud of her. She's leaving tomorrow night, and then we'll have to close up the place for good."

Before Julie knew what she was saying, she blurted, "I'm not."

The three of them stopped talking and gaped at her.

Julie swallowed and forced herself to say the words again, to really believe them. "I'm not leaving."

"Oh my goodness!"

Out of nowhere, Ivy launched herself into the huddle. Julie had no idea where she'd come from, but clearly, she'd overheard. Julie found the life squeezed out of her. She wheezed.

"Ivy…"

Her friend pulled back but didn't let go of Julie's arm. Her eyes were bright. "You're staying? Will you run the inn? This is fantastic! Why didn't you tell me sooner?"

"I hadn't made up my mind until now," Julie muttered.

Her words were drowned out by Myrtle's exclamation. "This is perfect! You stay, Ida will stay, and that sweet little cat will have a home."

That sweet little cat was probably upstairs in Julie's room, or worse, the room where they'd laid out all the coats. Everyone would be going home with white cat hair.

Of everyone in their little circle, the only person who was silent was Nolan. Julie glanced at him but couldn't read his expression. Had his plea for her to stay been nothing more than a drunken impulse?

Or maybe he hadn't thought it all the way through. If she stayed, if Gram decided not to sell the inn, then Klaus would be out the deal he and Gram had put together. A deal that, by Nolan's silence, might be more important to him than Julie staying in town. And why wouldn't it be? They'd only reconnected for ten days. Although she'd thought there had been a connection there, what if she was wrong? That connection might not be strong enough.

Was she making a mistake?

She turned back to the others and blurted, "But I can't run the inn. We're selling to Klaus."

The look in Gram's eye turned mercenary. "You let me handle that."

Ivy wrapped her arm around Julie's shoulders and squeezed. "See? It'll all work out. This is the best Christmas gift ever!"

Julie laughed, though she felt breathless. "Good. Because I didn't get you anything else."

If she'd thought gossip traveled fast around the town before, while they were all gathered at the party, it was lightning-quick. Ivy stepped away to tell her husband the good news, and suddenly, Julie was swarmed with well-wishers isolating her from the rest of her friends.

Ned came up to give her a hearty handshake and promise to make room in his schedule if the Cozy Holly Inn needed any more repairs to the plumbing. Julie shook his hand, fingers limp, and wondered, *Am I making a mistake?*

Lucy exclaimed over the good news and promised free coffee while Julie was still getting the inn up and running. The offer of coffee was almost enough to center Julie, but her thoughts still ran wild. *My entire life is in Boston. Apartment, friends, job opportunities.*

Then again, what was she really leaving? An apartment along a traffic-filled route that didn't allow cats. Her closest friend, Cheryl, who would never have shown up time and time again to help her out like Ivy had this past week. If she was running the family inn, she could still write freelance or even start that book. She'd finally have the time and not have to spend all her creativity writing what someone else wanted. Then there was Nolan... but as much as she liked him, she couldn't uproot her life and move just for him. If she did this, it had to be for *her*.

An older woman who Julie knew by sight but couldn't quite name came up and asked after room availability for New Year's. "My daughter and her family are coming down, and I'm just not as young as I used to be. I can't be cleaning up after them. But if they can stay here…"

Julie stumbled out an answer. *Would* the inn be ready to run by New Year's? She just didn't know. She had never done anything as ambitious as running an inn.

What if I move here and try and fail and we have to close up anyway?

Myrtle elbowed her way back into the throng at the front of the group of well-wishers. "Where is Ida?"

"I… I don't know." Julie scanned the room. Where was Gram?

Myrtle simply nodded and disappeared from the room, leaving Julie adrift among near strangers peppering her with questions. But Myrtle's question had grounded her, had reminded her of one important thing: *I'm not doing this alone.* No, she had Gram. Gram, who Julie had considered her personal superwoman growing up. Gram, who knew this inn like the back of her hand but just couldn't do it herself. And if Julie stayed with Gram, she would be able to capitalize on the time Gram had left. She was eighty, after all.

"Didn't Ida tell me you had a hot-shot interview back in Boston soon?"

At this point, Julie's head was spinning so much she couldn't even pinpoint who had asked the question. She needed air. She needed a minute to herself. As if from a distance, she heard herself answer, "I've decided not to take the job."

Julie's mom, with her vibrant personality and bright clothing, pulled Julie out of the corner and into the hall, where she was able to get some breathing room. It was clear the bulk of the partygoers still wanted to tender their congratulations at the news, but they held off as Julie's parents closed ranks around her.

"Did I hear Gram right? Are you staying in Pinecone Falls?"

At this point, it sounded almost surreal, like a dream. But every time she repeated it, it became more and more real. "I think so. If Gram can get out of selling the inn, I will."

Dad looked relieved. "Good. I've been worried about Gram. It will be better for her health if she keeps active, and I know that she hasn't been enjoying retirement."

That was definitely one point in favor of the decision Julie had made. It would make Gram happy. And despite what she'd thought when she'd arrived here ten days ago, it would make Julie happy too. Boston didn't hold as much appeal to her anymore.

Mom said, "I never liked you being in Boston, anyway."

The sound Julie made was one of half disbelief and half laughter. "Mom! You're always off to big cities all over the world."

"Yes, but I don't settle down in them for a reason. You've always thrived in Pinecone Falls. It used to be your favorite place in the world."

With a smile, Julie said, "Maybe it can still be that."

❄

NOLAN FELT LIKE HE WAS BALANCING ON A tightwire. The difference between Julie staying, where they could get to know each other and see where their relationship led from there, rested with how stubborn Gramps was going to be about this sale. Two weeks ago, Nolan would never have imagined that Gramps would let the Cozy Holly Inn and surrounding property go without an ugly fight. But the Gramps of two weeks ago was not the man who had offered up his kitchen to save the Christmas Eve party.

What had Ida Green said to him when they'd spoken privately? Nolan might never know. Nor would he know the magic that old woman had wrought in just fifteen minutes. It boggled the mind. Nolan stood on the threshold of the kitchen, agog at what he saw. He had to find Julie.

She was surrounded by people when he found her, but he had no compunction about wading in between, making his excuses, and tugging Julie out by the hand. It earned him some knowing looks, but so what? If all went well, they would be dating soon, and the entire town would know about it anyway.

The click of her heels followed him as he led her closer to the kitchen. As the crowd thinned and they found a moment of privacy, he turned to face her. Julie looked bewildered, paler than usual. Had she changed her mind? Stuffing away his excitement at the possibilities ahead, Nolan dropped her hand.

"You were so excited for your interview only a couple of hours ago. What changed?"

Her eyelashes fluttered in front of her eyes as she blinked slowly, processing the question. As much as he wanted her to answer that he was the reason, that she wanted to explore this thing between them as much as he did, he was simultaneously afraid of the answer.

Her smile chased away his lingering fears, and he found himself answering her in kind.

"Honestly, I think it was Pinecone Falls. I think it's been sneaking up on me this entire time. I feel happy, grounded. Like I used to when I visited over the summers."

He smirked and leaned closer. "A little differently, I hope."

She blushed furiously enough to match her dress.

As much as he wanted to kiss her in that moment, instead, he caught her by the hand and tugged her toward the kitchen. "You won't believe what our grandparents are doing."

When he and Julie stopped in the threshold to the kitchen, they found Ida and Gramps in the same scene as he'd left them. The pair were sitting at the small kitchen table, heads bent together as they toasted each other with what looked like the whiskey Gramps kept for special occasions. Outside, the jingle of sleigh bells as the sleigh passed with party-goers gave a clue as to how the whiskey had likely arrived.

Julie giggled and leaned against Nolan. He slipped his arm around her waist, but the private moment didn't last long. The sound caught the attention of their grandparents.

Ida announced, "It's all settled."

Nolan was afraid to celebrate. He looked at Gramps for confirmation.

The old man was smiling. "We've decided to do things a bit different. Instead of a buyout, we've decided to partner and coordinate to give our clientele the best experience we can."

"After all," Ida added, "the two inns have very different experiences. There's only one thing left to settle."

"What's that?" Julie asked. She sounded breathless. If he hadn't been touching her, he might not have been able to notice the tension vibrating through her. Excitement or apprehension?

Ida said, "After we pass, the businesses will be going to you and Nolan. Do you think you two will be able to work together?"

Nolan exchanged a glance with Julie. She was smiling. "Yeah," he said dryly. "I think we can manage that."

"Good," Gramps said with none of his usual curmudgeonly grumbles. In fact, he looked downright mischievous with the twinkle in his eye. "Then why don't you two make it official with a kiss? You're standing underneath the mistletoe."

Julie flushed again as she turned to him. This wasn't the way Nolan had envisioned their first kiss, but he wasn't about to turn away the opportunity

MEREDITH SUMMERS

either. Cupping her face, he leaned down and pressed his lips to hers.

When they separated, he found that one more person had snuck up behind them to join the party. Myrtle beamed. "Look at you two! So, everything's settled?"

Julie hesitated before she stepped away from Nolan to make room for Myrtle to enter the room. Nolan felt the same reluctance to part. But now that Julie was staying in town, they would have many more chances to kiss—and away from so many prying eyes.

Ida said, "Everything's settled. Julie and I will be running the Cozy Holly Inn together!"

"That's wonderful. And would you look at that." Myrtle gestured toward the white cat sprawled in front of one of the cabinets. "It looks as though someone has found his forever home."

Julie glanced at the cat, at her grandmother, and then finally at Nolan. Still meeting his gaze, she murmured, "I think that goes for two of us."

****

334

I HOPE YOU ENJOYED YOUR VISIT TO PINECONE FALLS! If you're looking for something to read next, you might like The Beachcomber Motel - Book 1 in the Shell Cove series of sweet small town women's fiction with a splash of romance:

ABOUT THE AUTHOR

Meredith Summers writes cozy mysteries as USA Today Bestselling author Leighann Dobbs and crime fiction as L. A. Dobbs.

She spent her childhood summers in Ogunquit Maine and never forgot the soft soothing feeling of the beach. She hopes to share that feeling with you through her books which are all light, feel-good reads.

Join her newsletter for sneak peeks of the latest books and release day notifications:

https://lobsterbay1.gr8.com

This is a work of fiction.

None of it is real. All names, places, and events are products of the author's imagination. Any resemblance to real names, places, or events are purely coincidental, and should not be construed as being real.

CHRISTMAS AT COZY HOLLY INN

Copyright © 2021

Meredith Summers

http://www.meredithsummers.com

All Rights Reserved.

No part of this work may be used or reproduced in any manner, except as allowable under "fair use," without the express written permission of the author.

❀ Created with Vellum